Lost in the Meantime

By Allasandra Buckner

To Jacob, you deserved a better story.

ALSO BY ALLASANDRA BUCKNER

Vicariously

Blood in the Algorithm

Chapter 1

The scent of lilies and freshly polished wood filled the air, thick and suffocating. The funeral home was packed, yet the silence was deafening. Muffled voices and quiet sobs wove together, forming a melody of grief that settled deep in my bones. I stood at the front, motionless, my fingers gripping the folded funeral program so tightly the paper threatened to tear.

A Ceremony of Life. That's what they called it. As if putting a different name to death made it any less unbearable. As if words could soften the sharp edges of reality. My stomach churned. My lungs burned. I wasn't sure I could do this.

Chapter 2

A hand rested gently on my arm. Ceci. Her touch was light, her presence grounding, but I couldn't bring myself to look at her. I knew if I did, I might fall apart completely. Instead, I focused on the polished mahogany casket, the final resting place of someone I had once known, someone whose absence pressed against my chest like a crushing weight.

I never expected to meet him that night.

"Just one game, Jules. Come on." Ceci's voice was playful, but I could hear the undercurrent of insistence in it. "You need to do something other than work and school."

I sighed, shifting in my chair. My TV screen glowed in the dimly lit room, **Fortnite's** loading screen flickering as I hesitated. "You know I suck at this game."

"That's what makes it fun! Now get on." Ceci sent me a game invite before I could protest further. With a resigned sigh, I clicked accept.

A new voice crackled through my headset. "You actually convinced her? Damn, Ceci, you must have some serious persuasion skills."

I frowned. "Who's this?"

"Relax," Ceci said, amusement lacing her words. "Jules, meet Jackson. Jackson, meet Jules."

"Hey, Jules," Jackson greeted, his voice warm and easy. "Hope you're ready to get carried."

I scoffed. "Excuse you? I may suck, but I am *not* dead weight."

Jackson laughed, and the sound was effortless, like he laughed easily and often. "We'll see about that."

The match started, and before I knew it, I was fully immersed. We fought. We won. We lost. And somewhere in between, the world outside my screen faded away. It finally felt like the for first time in a long time, I wasn't drowning in my own thoughts.

I didn't know it yet, but that night changed everything.

CHAPTER 3

Somewhere in the background, music played softly- The Kid LAROI. The familiarity of it sliced through me like a blade. My vision blurred, memories clawing at the edges of my mind.

It didn't take long for that one match to turn into something more. What had started as a distraction- a way to escape the exhaustion of work, school, and the relentless weight of my past- became a nightly ritual.

Every evening, after the last table was wiped down at the brewery, after my coursework was submitted in the dull glow of my laptop screen, I logged in. And Jackson was always there.

At first, it was just games. Mindless, competitive fun that had nothing to do with the real world. But over time, our conversations stretched between matches, filling the silences with something more substantial. Something *real*.

"You're getting better," Jackson teased one night, his voice crackling through my headset.

"Oh, so I was dead weight before?" I shot back, smirking despite myself.

"Didn't say that," Jackson chuckled. "But let's be real- you were definitely getting carried."

Ceci, who had been half-asleep during the match, let out an exaggerated snore. "God, can you two flirt somewhere else?"

"Flirt?" I repeated, scoffing, though my pulse quickened. "It's called banter."

"Mmhmm," Ceci hummed knowingly. "Keep telling yourself that."

But later that night, when it was just Jackson and me in the lobby, the words lingered. *Flirting*.

I didn't let myself think too hard about it. Not then.

"Rough day?" Jackson asked, his voice quieter now.

I hesitated, my fingers playing over the keys of my controller. "Yeah. Work sucked. School sucked. Everything sucked."

"You wanna talk about it?"

No one ever asked me that. Not really. Not in a way that felt like they actually wanted to hear the answer. No one but Ceci.

I sighed, leaning back in my chair. "Not much to talk about. Just exhausted."

"I get that," he said. "Sometimes life just kicks your ass."

"Pretty much."

Jackson was silent for a moment. Then he said, "Well, at least here, you don't have to think about all that."

I exhaled slowly. "Yeah. Here, I can just play."

And in that moment, that was enough.

But it didn't stop there.

Over the next few weeks, our conversations stretched beyond the game. It started with small things- what we liked to eat, the worst movies we'd ever seen, our mutual love for late-night drives with the windows down. Then, slowly, it became deeper.

I learned that Jackson had always wanted to move somewhere new, but never had the push to leave. That he had a complicated family dynamic, but never let it define him. That he loved music but didn't think he was good enough to pursue it seriously.

And somehow, he pulled pieces of me out that I hadn't shared with anyone else in a long time.

"If you could do anything, anything at all, and not fail," Jackson asked one night, "what would it be?"

I hesitated. "I don't know. I've always just... done what I was supposed to do."

"That's not an answer."

I rolled my eyes. "Fine. I guess I'd write. Maybe a book."

Jackson's voice brightened. "That's actually really cool. What would it be about?"

I blinked at the screen, caught off guard. No one had ever *asked* me that. It was always just a passing thought- something I'd never said out loud.

"I don't know yet," I admitted. "But I'd want it to mean something. I'd want it to *matter.*"

Jackson was quiet for a beat. Then he said, "I think you could do it."

Something about the way he said it made me believe it.

CHAPTER 4

I forced myself to swallow past the lump in my throat. I couldn't do this. Not now. Not here.

Reality felt different now, like I was living in two separate worlds. The days were long, filled with lectures I could barely focus on, the endless clatter of dishes at the brewery, and the exhaustion that seeped into my bones from running between school and work. But at night, none of that existed. At night, I logged in, and there was only *Fortnite*- only Jackson.

I wasn't sure when it started feeling like more than a game. Maybe it was the consistency, the way he was always there. Maybe it was the sound of his voice, steady and warm, cutting through the loneliness I didn't want to acknowledge. Maybe it was the way he never pushed, never asked for more than I could give. He was just there, a constant presence in a life that had always felt like it was slipping through my fingers.

Some nights, I caught myself waiting for his invite before I even opened the game, anticipation curling in my chest like something dangerous. I told myself it was just the routine, the comfort of familiarity. But deep down, I knew it was more than that.

One night, after Ceci logged off early, it was just me and Jackson left in the party lobby. The match countdown ticked down, and I could hear him shifting slightly on his end of the mic before he spoke.

"Hey, Jules."

"Yeah?"

"Do you ever feel like you're living two different lives? Like, the one you have to survive in and the one where you actually get to be yourself?"

I hesitated, fingers tightening around my controller. The weight of the question settled over me like a blanket, suffocating and exposing all at once. "Yeah. All the time."

"I figured. You work too much."

I snorted. "Says the guy who's between jobs."

"Touché," he chuckled. "But seriously, if you could do anything, no limits, no responsibilities- what would you do?"

The question threw me off. What *would* I do? It had been so long since I thought about what I actually wanted. Life had been about surviving- getting through school, making money, paying bills. Not dreaming.

"I don't know," I admitted. "I don't think I've let myself think about that."

"Maybe you should."

I swallowed hard. The idea of *wanting* something just for myself felt foreign, indulgent. Dangerous. "What about you?"

Jackson didn't hesitate. "Music."

I blinked. "Music?"

"Yeah. I'd drop everything and just- make music. Write, produce, sing. Whatever it takes."

There was something in his voice, something raw and honest that made my chest ache. The Jackson I knew- the easygoing, joke-cracking guy who could make me laugh even on my worst days- had this *depth* I hadn't seen before.

"You sing?"

"I mean, yeah. Not professionally or anything. But it's the only thing that's ever really felt right."

I let that sink in. Jackson- the guy who spent hours playing *Fortnite*, cracking jokes, making me forget how exhausted I was- had this whole other dream. Something real. Something beyond a game.

"I'd like to hear you sing sometime."

He was quiet for a moment before letting out a soft laugh. "I sing all the time."

I thought about that. Had I just never noticed? Or had I never paid attention? It made me wonder what else I'd overlooked in my life, what pieces of myself I'd buried beneath responsibilities and expectations.

"Maybe one day I'll write a book, and you can write the soundtrack for it," I joked, though the words felt oddly significant as I said them.

Jackson chuckled. "Deal."

The match loaded in, and we dropped onto the island. But my mind wasn't on the game anymore.

I started wondering what it would feel like to *chase* something, not just survive.

Maybe it was time I figured that out.

Chapter 5

My fingers trembled against the paper in my hands, my heart pounding in a disjointed rhythm. I inhaled sharply and forced myself to look up, my gaze locking onto the casket once more.

The thought of meeting Jackson in person settled into my mind like an idea I wasn't ready to name yet. It was there, lingering, waiting for me to acknowledge it. But acknowledging it meant admitting that this- whatever *this* was- mattered to me in a way that scared me.

I had spent so long surviving, keeping my guard up, convincing myself that wanting something was dangerous. Wanting led to disappointment. Wanting led to Cory.

But Jackson wasn't Cory.

I repeated that thought over and over again, like if I said it enough times, it would sink into my bones and make me believe it.

Work at the brewery was relentless that night. The crowd was rowdy, the tips were bad, and the exhaustion settled into my muscles long before I clocked out. By the time I got home, all I wanted to do was collapse. But instead, I found myself reaching for my laptop, logging in like I always did.

Jackson: *Thought you might bail on me tonight.*

I smirked at my screen. **Me:** *Please, you'd be lost without me.*

Jackson: *You're not wrong.*

The game loaded, and just like every night, the weight on my shoulders eased as soon as I heard his voice in my headset. There was something about the way he spoke, the way he made me laugh even when I thought I had nothing left to give.

We played for hours, like always, but somewhere between the late-night matches and the quiet conversations in between, something shifted. I could feel it in the pauses, in the way neither of us rushed to fill the silence.

"Hey, Jules?" Jackson's voice was softer now.

"Yeah?"

"I think I want to meet you."

My fingers froze on the controller. My heartbeat stuttered.

I had *thought* about it before, of course I had. But hearing him say it out loud made it real in a way I wasn't sure I was ready for.

"Oh," I said dumbly.

Jackson let out a quiet laugh. "Not exactly the reaction I was hoping for."

I exhaled, pressing my forehead into my hand. "I just- wasn't expecting that."

"Me either," he admitted. "But I feel like I already know you, and I guess... I want to know you outside of this too."

I bit my lip, hesitating. I wanted this- I *knew* I did. But wanting meant opening a door I had spent years keeping locked.

"Juliette?" Jackson's voice was cautious now, like he could sense my hesitation.

I swallowed past the fear in my throat and forced myself to be brave. "Yeah. I'd like that."

The silence that followed wasn't heavy. It wasn't filled with doubt. It was something else entirely.

Something real.

Chapter 6

I couldn't bring myself to step closer. Couldn't bring myself to look inside.

Because if I did, there would be no pretending anymore.

Jackson's words- *I think I want to meet you* lingered in my mind, but they weren't the only ones. Lately, the past had been creeping in, threading itself into the quiet moments I spent alone, refusing to let me move forward without a fight.

I should have been happy. Jackson made me feel like myself again, like I was more than just someone clawing their way through the wreckage. And yet, every time I let myself feel something real, Cory's voice echoed in my head, dragging me back into the past.

Cory had been intoxicating at first. The way he laughed, the way he knew exactly what to say to make me feel like I was the most important thing in the world. I was only nineteen when we got married, swept up in a love that felt like it could withstand anything. He had a confidence about him that made me feel safe, like I had finally found someone who would take care of me. And in the beginning, he did.

At first, there were flowers just because, long drives with our hands intertwined, whispered promises about forever. He knew all the right things to say, how to hold me in a way that made me believe every word. I remember looking at him one night, the moonlight casting a glow over his face, and thinking- *this is it. This is what love is supposed to feel like.*

But love shouldn't leave you hollow. It shouldn't be something you have to beg for.

The first time he cheated, I told myself it was a mistake. I forgave him. I believed the apologies, the pleading. *It won't happen again, I swear.* And for a while, things were good again. He kissed me the way he used to, touched me like I was something fragile, something worth holding onto. I clung to that version of him, convinced that if I just loved him enough, I could keep him that way.

The second time, I blamed myself. I wasn't affectionate enough. I was too distracted by school. I wasn't the girl he had fallen in love with anymore. Maybe if I dressed differently, acted differently, did more- *maybe then he'd stop looking for something else.*

By the third time, I knew the truth- Cory never saw me as a person. I was security, a provider, someone to cook his meals and keep the lights on while he chased whatever new thrill caught his eye. He would always love the idea of me, the stability I gave him, but he would never truly love *me*.

I stayed. Even when I found messages on his phone, even when I saw his eyes linger on other women the way they used to linger on me. Because leaving felt impossible. Because I was twenty-two and I had spent years believing we were forever. Because he had taken so much from me already, and I didn't know if I had anything left to start over with.

"Juliette?" Ceci's voice cut through my thoughts. I blinked, realizing I had been gripping the edge of the bar so tightly my knuckles were white.

She frowned, setting down the rag she had been using to wipe the counter. "You okay?"

I forced a nod, but my throat felt tight. "Yeah. Just tired."

She didn't believe me. I could tell by the way she watched me, studying the exhaustion in my face. "You were thinking about him again, weren't you?"

I exhaled, slumping against the counter. "I don't know how to stop."

"You don't just stop," Ceci said gently. "You make a choice. To stop letting him own space in your head. To stop giving him power over you when he's not even here."

I swallowed hard, hating that she was right.

The problem was, moving on wasn't as easy as people made it sound. It wasn't just about forgetting- it was about *reprogramming* myself to believe I deserved better. That I wasn't the reason he cheated. That I wasn't the problem.

I could still hear his voice sometimes, especially in moments like this. *You're overreacting, Jules. It didn't mean anything.*

Except it did. It had always meant something. Just not to him.

Ceci sighed, leaning against the counter beside me. "I know it's not easy. But you don't owe him anything- not your time, not your thoughts. He's not here anymore, Juliette. You are. And you have a whole life ahead of you."

I looked at her, wanting to believe her words. But believing something and *feeling* it were two different things.

"I just don't know how to let go," I admitted, my voice barely above a whisper.

"Then don't start by letting go," she said simply. "Start by holding on to something else. Something better."

My phone buzzed, breaking the moment.

Jackson: *Hey, you on tonight?*

I stared at the message, at the way my heart reacted instantly. It was easy, slipping into this routine of gaming, talking, letting him be my escape. But was it still just an escape? Or was it something more?

I thought about the weight of the past, how much it had taken from me, how much I had let it take.

Maybe Ceci was right. Maybe it was time to start choosing differently.

I picked up my phone and started typing.

Me: *Yeah. I'll be on soon.*

I wanted something more than just escape.

I wanted to see where this could lead.

Chapter 7

"No one knew the pain he hid and the struggles he went through..." one of his uncles took the podium and started to drone on about the amazing person he was.

The past didn't let go easily. It clung to me like smoke, lingering in the corners of my mind, slipping into my quietest moments when I least expected it.

Jackson wanted to meet. That thought should've filled me with excitement, but instead, it unraveled something uneasy inside me. What if

I had built this whole connection in my head? What if, in the real world, I wasn't enough?

Cory had once made me feel like I was. In the beginning, at least. He had promised forever, whispered dreams of a life that never materialized. But those whispers turned into excuses. Those dreams turned into lies.

It wasn't just the infidelity. It was the slow erosion of who I was. The manipulation disguised as love. The way he convinced me that I was *lucky* to have him, that I wasn't the kind of girl other men would want. And I had believed him. I had swallowed his words whole until they became my own thoughts.

The night I caught him for the last time, it wasn't even a grand revelation. There were no screaming matches, no shattered plates. Just cold, undeniable proof- financial statements, hotel charges, and the messages I shouldn't have had to see.

I had stood in the kitchen, staring at the receipts in my shaking hands, waiting for him to at least *try* to lie. But he didn't. He just shrugged.

"You always knew what I was," he said simply, as if that was supposed to make it hurt less.

I had walked out that night and never looked back. At least, that's what I told myself. But the truth was, a part of me had never left that kitchen. A part of me was still standing there, holding those receipts, realizing that the love I had fought for had never really been mine.

"Earth to Jules," Ceci's voice yanked me back to the present. I blinked, realizing I had been scrubbing the same spot on the bar for far too long.

"Sorry," I muttered, setting the rag down.

She studied me for a long moment. "You sure you want to do this?"

"Do what?"

"Meet Jackson."

I hesitated. Did I? Or was I just convincing myself that I did?

"I don't know," I admitted. "What if it's different? What if I've made this whole thing up in my head?"

Ceci leaned against the counter, folding her arms. "Or what if it's *exactly* what you need?"

I sighed, rubbing my temples. "I just don't want to be that girl again. The one who falls too fast, who trusts too easily."

"You're not her anymore," Ceci said, her voice firm. "And Jackson is *not* Cory."

I swallowed hard. I wanted to believe that. More than anything, I wanted to believe that.

My phone buzzed. **Jackson:** *Still up for tonight?*

I stared at the message, my heart pounding in my chest.

Maybe Ceci was right. Maybe it was time to take a risk.

    I picked up my phone and started typing.
Me: *Yeah. Let's do this.*

Chapter 8

"I never met a harder worker…"

The anxiety settled deep in my stomach as I sat on the edge of my bed, my phone still clutched in my hands. I had said yes. I had agreed to see Jackson. And now, there was no taking it back.

It wasn't just nerves- it was fear. Of what, I wasn't sure. Maybe that the connection we had built would shatter once we were face-to-face. Maybe that he'd take one look at me and see someone different from the version of me he knew online.

Or maybe, worst of all, that he was everything I had imagined, and I wouldn't know what to do with that.

Ceci paced in the doorway, her arms crossed. "You're overthinking again."

"I'm not overthinking," I muttered. "I'm just... thinking."

"Jules," she sighed, dropping onto the bed beside me. "You've spent months talking to him, laughing with him, trusting him. You wouldn't be this scared if you didn't know, deep down, that it's real."

I swallowed. "I want to believe that."

"Then believe it. Jackson is a good guy."

The simplicity of her words frustrated me. I had spent years second-guessing myself, my choices, my own worth. It wasn't that easy to just *believe*.

But maybe she was right. Maybe it was time to stop expecting the worst and start hoping for something better.

My phone buzzed again. **Jackson:** *I can't drive out. My car's in the shop. Still up for coming here?*

I stared at the message, my stomach twisting. I had expected to meet him somewhere neutral, on equal ground. But now, I'd be the one stepping fully into his world.

Me: *Yeah. I'll leave in an hour.*

My hands shook slightly as I put my phone down. Ceci nudged my shoulder. "Go get ready. And stop looking like you're heading to your execution."

I let out a shaky breath and stood up, forcing myself toward the mirror. My reflection stared back, wide-eyed and uncertain. I smoothed down my hair, straightened my shirt, and exhaled again.

I could do this.

I *would* do this.

The drive stretched endlessly before me. Three hours of highway, of too much time to think, of second-guessing every decision that had led to this moment. The sun dipped lower as the miles passed, the sky shifting to warm hues of gold and orange.

    I cycled through music, stopping when **The Kid LAROI** came on, my fingers gripping the steering wheel tighter. Jackson and I had played this song together more times than I could count. I could almost hear him humming along in my headset, a bit loud, but unbothered.

    Would he be different in person? Would I?

    A familiar panic crept in, the kind that whispered, *You're making a mistake. Turn around. Stay safe.* But this wasn't a mistake. I knew that deep down, no matter how terrified I was.

    When I finally pulled off the highway, my nerves were a tangled mess. The town was bigger than mine, not a sprawling city, but still unfamiliar. The GPS led me through winding streets until I reached his apartment complex. It wasn't anything fancy- red brick, a second-floor balcony, the kind of place that looked lived-in but comfortable.

    I turned off the engine, gripping the steering wheel with clammy hands. What if he didn't like me in person? What if I wasn't what he expected? What if all of this came crashing down the second we stood face-to-face?

Then, the front door opened.

And I saw him.

Jackson was impossible to miss- 6'5, dark black hair that curled slightly at the ends, a lean but strong build, and a chiseled face that looked like it had been carved by something divine. His almond-shaped brown eyes scanned the parking lot, long lashes casting shadows against his cheekbones as he looked around. The second his gaze landed on my car, something shifted.

A slow, knowing smile spread across his lips, and before I could second-guess myself again, he jogged down the steps toward me. He moved with effortless confidence, his hands shoved into the pockets of his jacket, his posture relaxed. Like he wasn't nervous at all.

I inhaled sharply, my heart hammering. Then, with shaky hands, I grabbed my purse, pushed the car door open, and stepped into the cool evening air.

Jackson stopped a few feet away, studying me with an unreadable expression. For a split second, I was convinced I had made a mistake. That I had been safer when we were just voices through a headset.

Then, he grinned. "Hey, Jules."

Just like that, the fear melted away.

I wanted this. I wanted *him*.

Chapter 9

"There wasn't anything he wouldn't do for someone. You called and he was there..."

The air between us was charged, thick with something unspoken. Standing in front of Jackson, I felt stripped of the shield that had existed between us- the screens, the game, the distance. Now, there was no buffer, no way to hide behind carefully typed words or muted microphones.

He was real. More real than I had prepared for.

His grin softened as he studied me, like he was committing me to memory. "Long drive?"

I let out a shaky breath. "Felt longer than three hours."

"Worth it?" His voice held the familiar teasing edge I had grown so used to, but there was something else laced beneath it- something cautious.

I let my eyes wander over him, taking in the details I had only imagined before. The way his hair curled slightly, the sharp lines of his jaw, the way his hoodie sat slightly loose on his frame. His hands, now out of his pockets, hung at his sides like he wasn't quite sure what to do with them.

I exhaled slowly, nodding. "Yeah."

The tension cracked, just a little. He chuckled, running a hand through his hair. "Good. 'Cause I was about to be real embarrassed if you took one look at me and bailed."

I rolled my eyes. "If I wanted to bail, I wouldn't have spent three hours on the road."

"Fair point." He gestured toward the stairs leading to his apartment. "Wanna come up? Or do you need a minute to talk yourself out of it first?"

I hesitated, my fingers tightening around the strap of my bag. It wasn't about nerves anymore. It was about *crossing that final line*. Once I walked through his door, there would be no more wondering, no more what-ifs.

I squared my shoulders. "I'm good. Let's go."

His apartment was exactly what I expected- lived-in, a little messy, but comfortable. A gaming setup in the corner, wires snaking from the desk to the console, a guitar propped against the wall, and an open bag of chips left abandoned on the coffee table. It smelled like something warm, like soap and cologne, a scent that was distinctly *him*.

"Sorry about the mess," Jackson muttered, kicking a pair of sneakers out of the walkway. "I was gonna clean, but, y'know... anxiety."

I smirked, setting my bag down. "I expected worse."

"Oh, don't give me that much credit. You haven't seen my closet yet."

He motioned toward the couch, and I sat down, suddenly aware of how close we were. In-game, we were always connected- our voices filling each other's headsets, our movements synchronized on-screen. But here, in person, the space between us felt *louder*.

Jackson sat beside me, leaning back against the cushions, his knee just barely brushing mine. "So, Jules. We did it. We're actually in the same room."

I laughed, shaking my head. "Yeah. Kinda crazy, huh?"

"A little bit." He exhaled, stretching his arms over the back of the couch. "You hungry? I could order something. Or, if you're feeling brave, I could cook."

I raised an eyebrow. "Define 'cook.'"

"Uh, I make a mean grilled cheese. And by 'mean,' I mean *barely edible*."

I laughed, shaking my head. "Let's go with ordering."

Jackson grinned. "Good call."

He grabbed his phone, scrolling through options while I took a second to absorb everything. This- being here with him, sitting on his couch, watching him exist in the same space as me- it felt surreal. Like I was still in some alternate reality where I had stepped outside of my own life and landed somewhere else entirely.

But it didn't feel wrong.

It felt... right.

Jackson glanced at me between menu selections. "Hey, Jules?"

"Yeah?"

He hesitated, then smirked. "Don't make it weird, but I'm really glad you came."

I smiled. "Me too."

Chapter 10

"I never thought we would lose someone so young, so fast..."

The takeout containers sat half-eaten on the coffee table, the remnants of a meal neither of us had really been focused on. The TV played some random show in the background, but I wasn't paying attention.

I was too focused on the way Jackson's knee still brushed against mine, on the way his fingers absentmindedly traced the rim of his drink, on the way his body seemed closer than before- whether intentional or not, I couldn't tell.

I had never been good at moments like this. The ones that felt suspended in time, where something *more* was hovering between us, just out of reach.

Jackson shifted, turning slightly to face me. "Okay, serious question."

I smirked. "Hit me."

"Do you still think I sound different in person?"

I laughed, shaking my head. "Not different. Just... more real."

"More real, huh?" He grinned, but there was something in his expression- something softer, something *intentional*.

I felt it before I even realized what was happening. The space between us shrinking. His hand moving slightly, fingertips grazing mine. The warmth of his skin sent a shiver through me, and suddenly, every nerve in my body was on high alert.

He was close now, closer than before. His voice was lower when he spoke again. "Jules."

"Yeah?" My voice came out quieter than I expected.

"Can I kiss you?"

My stomach flipped, a slow burn spreading through my chest at the way he asked- like he wanted to be sure, like he wouldn't cross a line unless I wanted him to.

I swallowed, then nodded. "Yeah."

Jackson didn't rush. He moved slowly, giving me time to back away if I wanted to. But I didn't. I couldn't.

The moment his lips met mine, everything else faded. His hand came up to cup my jaw, his thumb grazing my cheek in a way that sent warmth straight through me. The kiss was soft at first- tentative, testing- but then I leaned into him, and he responded in kind, his fingers threading through my hair, pulling me in deeper.

I melted against him, letting myself fall into the moment, into *him*.

When we finally pulled apart, his forehead rested against mine, his breath warm against my skin. "That was..."

I let out a breathless laugh. "Yeah."

Jackson grinned, his hand still cradling my face. "Wanna do it again?"

I smirked, my fingers curling into the fabric of his hoodie. "Absolutely."

And so we did.

I don't know how long we sat there, tangled in each other. Kissing. Talking. Letting our walls drop one careful inch at a time. Jackson's fingers traced lazy circles against the inside of my wrist as we lay side by side on the couch, legs tangled like we had been doing this forever.

"I still can't believe you're actually here," he murmured, his voice heavy with something between exhaustion and contentment.

"Me neither," I admitted. "This whole thing... feels surreal."

He exhaled a quiet laugh. "Good surreal or *what-the-hell-am-I-doing* surreal?"

"Good surreal," I said immediately. "Definitely good surreal."

Jackson's thumb brushed over my knuckles, a quiet, thoughtful movement. "Can I be honest?"

"I hope so."

He hesitated, and then, "I was terrified before you got here."

I turned to look at him, surprised. "You? Terrified?"

"Yeah." He gave me a sheepish grin. "Not that I thought you'd hate me or anything, but... I don't know. You were kind of this *untouchable* thing in my head. This person I only knew in pieces- your voice, your laugh, the way you totally throw our Fortnite matches when you panic- "

"I do *not* throw- "

"You do, but I forgive you," he teased. "Point is, I didn't know if it would feel the same in person."

I bit my lip. "And?"

He squeezed my hand. "It feels *better*. You are more beautiful than I could have ever imagined."

Something about the way he said it made my heart squeeze. No hesitation. No teasing. Just truth.

I let my head rest against his shoulder, my fingers tracing the hem of his sleeve.

We stayed like that, wrapped up in a silence that didn't need to be filled. The kind of silence that felt safe.

I let myself believe this- *whatever this was*- was real.

Chapter 11

His uncle stopped talking for a moment and the room went silent, apart from the low-fi music playing in the background. He cleared his throat and continued...

The night stretched on, but neither of us made a move to break away. The low hum of the TV blended into the quiet city sounds outside the window, the distant honking of a car, the muffled voices of people passing on the street below. The world outside kept moving, but in here, wrapped up in Jackson's warmth, it felt like time had paused.

He traced patterns on my wrist, his touch absentminded but deliberate. I could feel the heat of his skin through my sleeve, the lazy way his fingers moved like he was memorizing me. Every small gesture, every little movement, felt new and electrifying. I wasn't used to this- to being *seen* in such an unhurried, careful way.

"What's going on in that head of yours?" he murmured.

I sighed, shifting slightly so I could look at him. "I don't know. I guess I'm just... waiting for this to not feel real."

His lips quirked. "It *is* real, Jules."

I swallowed. "I know. But you- this- I don't know. It almost feels too good to be true."

Jackson's expression softened, his brown eyes studying me like he was peeling back the layers I didn't even realize I had. "You've been through some shit, huh?"

I let out a dry laugh. "That obvious?"

"Kind of." He brushed a strand of hair behind my ear, his touch featherlight. "You don't have to say it if you don't want to. But if you do, I'll listen."

That was the thing about Jackson. He never *pushed*. He never demanded more than I was willing to give. With Cory, love had felt like an obligation, like a never-ending checklist of things I had to do just to be *enough*. But with Jackson, there was no expectation. Just space. Just patience.

I exhaled slowly. "It's not just the past. It's... me. I think I forgot how to do this. How to let something be *good* without waiting for it to go wrong."

Jackson nodded like he understood in a way few people did. "Maybe it's time to relearn."

I looked at him, really looked at him- the sharp jawline, the barely-there stubble, the warmth in his eyes. "Maybe."

He smirked. "No pressure, but I'm a pretty great teacher."

I rolled my eyes, but I couldn't stop the smile from tugging at my lips. "Oh yeah? What's your lesson plan?"

Jackson grinned, shifting so that he hovered just slightly over me, his hands braced on either side of my hips. "Step one: stop overthinking. Step two... kiss me again."

My breath hitched. "And step three?"

His voice dropped lower. "Guess you'll have to stick around and find out."

I laughed softly, shaking my head before closing the space between us again. This kiss was different than the first. Deeper. Unrushed. My fingers tangled in his hair, and I felt the way he sighed into me, like he had been waiting for this just as much as I had.

When we finally pulled apart, he rested his forehead against mine, his breath warm against my lips. "See? Told you I was a great teacher."

I bit my lip, my heart still hammering. "I might need extra lessons."

Jackson chuckled, his fingers tracing up my arm. "Good thing I don't mind tutoring."

We stayed wrapped up in each other for what felt like forever, talking about nothing and everything. We laughed, played music, made up ridiculous songs, and filled the apartment with a kind of warmth and happiness I hadn't felt in years. For a while, it felt easy, like we had all the time in the world.

But time wasn't something we could ignore forever.

The next morning, reality set in. My bag sat by the door, my keys resting on the counter beside Jackson's phone. The easy comfort of last night felt distant now, replaced by something heavier. Something uncertain.

Jackson leaned against the kitchen counter, arms crossed. "So, you heading out soon?"

I swallowed, nodding. "Yeah. Long drive. Work in the morning"

He nodded, but there was something unreadable in his expression. Something hesitant. I wanted him to say it- to ask me to stay, to tell me this was more than just a moment frozen in time.

Instead, he exhaled. "This was good, Jules. Really good."

I forced a smile. "Yeah, it was."

"You know I- " He paused, running a hand through his hair. "I don't really do labels. Not because I don't care, but... I don't know. I just don't want to mess this up."

My heart clenched, but I nodded. "I get it."

And I did. But that didn't make it any easier.

He stepped closer, his fingers brushing my wrist before he pulled me in for one last kiss. It was slower this time, more lingering, like he wanted me to feel it even after I was gone.

When we pulled away, he rested his forehead against mine. "We'll talk soon?"

I nodded, trying not to let the lump in my throat show. "Yeah. We'll talk soon."

But as I walked out the door, as I got into my car and watched his apartment fade in my rearview mirror, I couldn't shake the feeling that *talking* wouldn't be enough.

CHAPTER 12

"I know he made some enemies, but that doesn't matter right now. What matters is his life has come to an end, and we must grieve for now, so we can move on later..."

The drive back felt longer than the drive there. Maybe it was the exhaustion settling into my bones, or maybe it was the weight of everything I wasn't saying aloud. The way Jackson kissed me goodbye still lingered on my lips, and yet, the unspoken words between us sat heavier than ever.

I don't really do labels.

I had told him I understood. That I got it. And I did. But that didn't mean it didn't sting.

The problem wasn't that Jackson didn't care. If anything, he had shown me more care, more patience, more understanding than anyone had in years. But something about *us* scared him. Or maybe he just didn't want to claim something he wasn't sure of yet. Either way, I felt like I had left a part of myself back in his apartment, waiting for him to pick it up and decide what to do with it.

Ceci's text popped up on my screen as I stopped at a gas station halfway home.

Ceci: *Back yet?*

Me: *Almost.*

Ceci: *And?*

I hesitated, my fingers hovering over the screen before I finally typed back.

Me: *It was amazing. But... complicated.*

Ceci: *Complicated how?*

I didn't answer right away. Instead, I shoved my phone into my pocket and stepped out of the car, stretching my sore muscles. The cold air bit at my skin, but I welcomed it. Anything to clear my head.

The truth was, I didn't know how to explain it to Ceci without sounding ridiculous. Jackson and I had spent months talking, gaming, getting to know every little thing about each other. It felt like we had built something real, something solid. But now, I was beginning to wonder if I had read too much into it. If he had always seen this as something temporary, something fleeting.

My phone buzzed again.

Ceci: *Jules, don't overthink it. We will talk when you get home.*

I sighed, climbing back into the driver's seat. *Too late.*

By the time I pulled into my driveway, the sky had darkened, my body screaming for rest. But sleep wouldn't come easy tonight. I already knew that.

I showered, changed into an oversized hoodie, and collapsed onto my bed, staring at the ceiling. My phone sat next to me, silent. I told myself I wouldn't be the first one to text. That if Jackson wanted to talk, he would.

But an hour passed. Then two. And still-nothing.

My heart sank. He had said we would talk soon, but now that I was gone, had I already started fading from his mind?

I groaned, rolling onto my side, determined to ignore the gnawing doubt in my chest. But just as I closed my eyes, my phone lit up.

Jackson: *Made it home okay?*

I exhaled, relief mixing with frustration.

Me: *Yeah. Just tired.*

A few seconds later-

Jackson: *Same. Today was... really good, Jules.*

I hesitated before responding.

Me: *Yeah. It was.*

He didn't say anything else. No "good night," no reassurance, no acknowledgment of the storm that had been brewing inside me the entire ride home.

I set my phone down, staring at the ceiling once more.

If this was going to be enough for him, was it going to be enough for me?

Chapter 13

His uncle cleared his throat and left the podium, offering a few moments of silence. Just the ominous crowd and the casket in front of us.

Days passed, and Jackson kept his word- we talked. But something felt different. Not in the way people drift apart, but in the way distance seeps in like a slow leak, filling the spaces between words that once carried meaning.

Conversations that used to stretch into the early morning hours became shorter. Messages took longer to send. Calls that once felt effortless were now scheduled between obligations, excuses, and moments of silence I didn't know how to fill.

I tried to tell myself I was imagining it, that this was just what happened when people weren't physically together. But I knew better.

Ceci knew too.

"You're spiraling, Jules." Her voice was laced with concern as she lounged on the couch, watching me scroll through my last text thread with Jackson.

Me: *How's your day going?*
Jackson: *Pretty good, just busy. You?*
Me: *Same. Miss talking to you though.*
Jackson: *Yeah, me too. We'll catch up soon.*

But soon never came.

I locked my phone and sighed. "I don't know what's happening. One minute we were fine, and now... it's like he's slipping through my fingers."

Ceci tucked her legs beneath her. "Look, I know you don't want to hear this, but maybe he's just not in the same place you are."

"He kissed me like he was." My voice was quieter than I intended, like I was trying to convince myself more than her.

Ceci gave me a look, one I had seen before- *the truth-you-don't-want-to-face look*. "Feelings and timing don't always line up, Jules. Sometimes people just... aren't ready."

I swallowed, nodding even though my chest tightened at the thought. "So what do I do? Just wait for him to figure it out?"

"No." She sat forward. "You live your life. If he wants to be in it, he will. But don't put yourself on pause waiting for someone who won't hit play."

I wanted to argue. To say that it wasn't that simple. But maybe it was. Maybe the problem wasn't that I was losing Jackson- maybe it was that I had already lost myself trying to hold onto him.

That night, I lay in bed, phone resting on my chest, waiting for something- anything- from him.

Nothing came.

The longer I stared at the screen, the more foolish I felt. I had spent so much time believing that what we had was something untouchable, something worth holding onto. But maybe I was the only one who saw it that way.

With a deep breath, I typed out a message.

Me: *Are we okay?*

I hovered over the send button, my thumb trembling. I wanted to ask it out loud. To hear his voice, to feel the weight of his answer. But I already knew.

I deleted the message.

I let silence speak for itself.

Chapter 14

I let out a shaky breath as I watched people look around, waiting for the next person to go up and speak. I wanted to. God, I wanted to. But everything forced me to stop...

Winter break came faster than I expected, and with it, an opportunity I hadn't been sure I wanted. I had two full weeks off- no classes, no shifts at the brewery, nothing but time I wasn't sure how to fill.

And then Jackson texted.

Jackson: *You still up?*

It was past midnight, and I had been staring at the message for longer than I wanted to admit. I told myself I wasn't going to do this again- wait for him, let him dictate when we talked, when he showed up in my life. But something in me still ached for whatever this was, whatever we were.

Me: *Yeah, what's up?*

Jackson: *Any chance you wanna get away for a bit?*

I hesitated, rereading the words over and over.

Me: *Where?*

Jackson: *Here. For a while. I got a place lined up. No distractions. Just us.*

It was tempting. Dangerous, even. Because I knew what happened when we were together. The world shrank to just us, and everything else- doubt, reality, the distance- faded into the background. But then I'd go back, and the silence would creep in again.

And yet, despite everything, I found myself typing back.

Me: *I'll think about it.*

The drive felt different this time. Last time, I had been excited, nervous in the way that came from stepping into the unknown. But now, I was more cautious. I wasn't just walking into something fresh- I was walking into something unfinished.

Jackson met me outside, just like before. His hands were stuffed into the pockets of his jacket, dark curls falling slightly over his forehead. He was taller than I remembered- or maybe I had just forgotten what it felt like to stand beneath the weight of his gaze.

"You came," he said, a small smile tugging at his lips.

"Yeah." I shifted my bag on my shoulder. "I guess I did."

For a second, neither of us moved. Then, he let out a breath and took my bag from me, slinging it over his shoulder. "Come on. I'll show you the place."

Jackson hadn't been lying- the place was secluded, tucked away in a quiet neighborhood just outside of town. It was small but warm, a rental he had somehow managed to get for the break. A record player sat in the corner, an old guitar leaned against the couch, and blankets were piled on a worn-out recliner.

"It's nothing fancy," he said, setting my bag down by the door. "But it's ours for a while."

Ours.

I swallowed. "It's nice."

"Yeah?" He looked at me, something unreadable in his expression. "I just figured... I don't know. Maybe we needed this. Time."

"Time for what?" I asked, watching him carefully.

He hesitated before responding. "To just be. Without expectations. Without... pressure."

I nodded, even though I wasn't sure if I agreed or if I was just agreeing because it was easier.

That night, we didn't talk about *us*. Instead, we made music, played old records, let our voices mix and clash in harmonies that felt right. We laughed until our stomachs hurt, argued over which pizza toppings were acceptable, and ended the night curled up on the couch watching some movie neither of us paid attention to.

The days blurred together in a way that felt effortless. We woke up late, cooked breakfast in mismatched pajamas, and took long drives without a destination. Some nights, we stayed up playing music until dawn, our voices hoarse from singing too much. Other nights, we sat in silence, just existing in the same space, no words needed.

It felt easy. Too easy.

And I knew, deep down, that I couldn't stay in this suspended reality forever.

One night, we lay side by side on the couch, legs tangled, the glow of the TV washing over us. I turned my head toward him, watching as his fingers absentmindedly traced the hem of his hoodie.

"What are you thinking?" I asked quietly.

Jackson let out a small chuckle. "You always ask me that."

"Because you never say it unless I do."

He was quiet for a long time before he finally exhaled. "I like this, Jules. Being here. With you."

"But?" I prompted, sensing the hesitation.

His jaw tensed slightly. "But I don't know how to make it last."

"What do you mean?"

Jackson turned on his side to face me, his dark eyes searching mine. "I mean, I don't know how to be what you want me to be. I don't want to lose you, but I also don't want to rush into something if I'm not ready."

I swallowed hard. "So where does that leave us?"

"Here. Right now. Together." His hand brushed against mine, fingertips just barely touching. "Is that enough?"

I didn't answer right away because I wasn't sure. I wanted to say yes. I wanted to believe that being with him in whatever way I could was better than not being with him at all. But deep down, I knew the truth- *I wanted more.*

But I also wasn't ready to walk away.

So I took his hand and laced my fingers through his. "For now, it is."

Jackson smiled, but there was something in his eyes that made me wonder if he believed it any more than I did.

That night, I lay awake in bed, listening to the quiet rise and fall of his breathing from the other room. I had always thought that love- real love- would come with certainty, with the kind of clarity that left no room for doubt.

But maybe love wasn't always that simple.

Maybe, sometimes, it was about learning when to hold on.

And when to let go.

Chapter 15

I made my move to stand, but his mom beat me to it and I sat back down so quick. She slowly walked up to the podium, eyes red and puffy; I felt bad for her. Her hair was a mess, her once-normal composed self now looking distraught. I don't blame her.

The last morning in the rental felt different. The air between us was quieter, heavier, like we both knew something was coming but neither of us wanted to be the first to say it.

I sat on the edge of the bed, watching the way the sunlight poured through the thin curtains, cutting golden streaks across the wooden floor. I could hear Jackson moving around in the kitchen, the clinking of mugs, the low hum of a song I recognized but couldn't place.

It was easy to pretend that this was normal, that this was just another morning. But it wasn't.

Jackson appeared in the doorway, holding out a cup of coffee. "You look deep in thought."

I took the cup, wrapping my hands around the warmth. "Just thinking."

He smirked, leaning against the frame. "You do that a lot."

I sighed. "It's kind of my thing."

"You thinking about us?"

I looked up at him then, surprised by the directness of his question. Jackson wasn't usually the one to bring it up.

"Yeah," I admitted. "Are you?"

He nodded, running a hand through his hair before stepping further into the room. "I don't want this to end, Jules. But I also don't know how to keep it going."

I studied him, the way his eyes flickered with something hesitant. "Why does it have to be one or the other?"

"Because I don't want to hurt you," he said softly. "And I feel like I will, eventually."

My chest tightened. "What if I'm willing to take that risk?"

He let out a breath, setting his coffee down on the nightstand. "Then you're braver than me."

I swallowed hard, my throat burning. "Jackson-"

He sat down beside me, close but not touching. "I care about you, Jules. More than I know how to say. And maybe that's the problem. I've never been good at this- at letting myself have something real."

I turned toward him. "Then why did you ask me to come? Why do all of this if you weren't sure?"

"Because I *am* sure," he said, his voice barely above a whisper. "I just don't know if I'm ready."

Silence stretched between us, thick and unrelenting. I hated it. I hated that I understood him, that I knew exactly what he meant even when I wanted to fight against it.

I exhaled, looking down at my hands. "So what now?"

Jackson hesitated before reaching for my hand, threading his fingers through mine. "Now, we figure it out. One step at a time. No promises, no pressure. Just... us."

I squeezed his hand, my heart aching with the weight of his words. "Okay."

He lifted our joined hands and kissed my knuckles, his lips lingering against my skin. "Okay."

For now, I thought that was enough.

Later that afternoon, I packed my bag, moving slower than I needed to. Jackson watched me from the couch, his expression unreadable.

"You sure you don't want to stay a little longer?" he asked, only half-teasing.

I smiled, but it didn't quite reach my eyes. "Tempting. But I should probably get back to reality."

He nodded, but neither of us moved.

Finally, I sighed, stepping closer. "I'm going to miss this."

Jackson reached up, tugging me down onto the couch beside him. "Me too."

We sat there for a while, wrapped up in the warmth of something unspoken, something fragile but still whole. I rested my head against his shoulder, breathing him in, memorizing the way he felt.

When I finally stood to leave, he walked me to the door. "Drive safe, Jules."

"I will."

He hesitated, then leaned down, pressing a slow, lingering kiss against my lips. "We'll talk soon, yeah?"

I nodded, ignoring the way my heart twisted. "Yeah."

And then, with one last look, I walked away.

"Hey," he suddenly called out, "love you." He smiled.

My heart felt like gunfire. I couldn't help but smile and feel my cheeks warming up as I shyly called back, "Love you, too."

With that, I got in my car and drove off.

Chapter 16

"I know a lot of you knew my son. You knew different parts of him. Some knew him as the sweet, kind, caring boy, others as the life of the party. Whatever you knew him as, I just hope those memories resonate as good." His mom paused with tears in her eyes as she nodded and looked around, then continued.

The drive home was different this time. Quieter. The hum of the tires against the road filled the silence where my thoughts used to be loud, but now, all I could hear was Jackson's voice, soft and sure, repeating the last thing he said to me.

Love you.

And I had said it back.

It wasn't dramatic, or rushed, or filled with some grand declaration. It had slipped out of me like it had always been there, waiting. Like it was the easiest thing in the world to say because it had been true for so long, I just hadn't let myself admit it.

Love you too.

And then I had left.

Now, as the miles stretched between us, I wanted to turn around. To ask him what it meant. To ask him if he regretted saying it. But I kept driving.

I made it back home just as the sun started to set, the golden hues casting long shadows across the street. Ceci's car was already in my driveway. She must've been waiting for me.

I barely made it through the door before she pulled me into a tight hug. "So? How was it?" she asked, stepping back and scanning my face like she could read the entire week in my expression.

I swallowed hard, dropping my bag by the couch. "It was..."

Ceci raised an eyebrow. "That bad?"

"No, not bad." I sighed, running a hand through my hair. "It was amazing. But it was also confusing. And complicated."

She flopped onto the couch, patting the seat beside her. "Spill."

I sat down, pressing my hands together. "We had fun. We made music, we laughed, we did all the things we always do. But there's still this thing hanging between us- like he's scared to hold onto me, but even more scared to let me go."

Ceci frowned. "And you? What do you want?"

I hesitated. "I want him. I want him without the uncertainty. But I don't know if I can have that."

"Did you talk about it?"

I let out a dry laugh. "Jackson isn't much of a talker when it comes to feelings. But... he said something before I left."

She sat up straighter. "Yeah?"

I exhaled, my heart still stumbling over the words. "He told me he loves me. And I told him I love him too."

Ceci's eyes widened. "Wait. *What?*"

I nodded. "I said it back. And then I left."

She blinked at me, processing. "Jules."

"I know."

"Jules."

"*I know.*"

She ran a hand over her face. "So what now?"

I exhaled slowly, staring at my hands. "That's the thing. I don't know. Because I think he loves me in the way that *scares* him. And I don't know what to do with that."

Ceci was quiet for a long moment before finally speaking. "That's the thing about love, Jules. Sometimes it's not about who loves who more. It's about who's willing to *fight* for it."

Her words sat heavy in the air between us.

And for the first time since I left, I wondered if Jackson was willing to fight for me.

Or if I was the only one standing in the ring.

Chapter 17

"But I don't care what anyone says, my boy was a good boy!" His mom was shouting and sobbing. His uncle got up to comfort her. She waved him off and cleared her throat.

Days passed, and the weight of what had been said lingered in the quiet spaces between conversations. Jackson and I still talked, but there was something different now- something neither of us knew how to name.

Love had been spoken into existence, but love alone had never been enough to fix what was broken.

I found myself waiting for something to shift, for Jackson to say something more, to prove that this wasn't just another fleeting moment between us. But as time stretched on, I realized I might be waiting for something that would never come.

Ceci saw it too.

"You're thinking about him again," she said, handing me a cup of coffee as we sat on my porch. It wasn't a question. It was a statement. A fact.

I wrapped my hands around the warm ceramic, watching the steam curl into the cool evening air. "I don't know what to do."

Ceci exhaled, pulling her knees up to her chest, her red curls flowing in the wind. "What do you *want* to do?"

I swallowed. "I want him to show me that he meant it. That he's not just saying things because they feel right in the moment."

She nodded, taking a slow sip of her drink. "And if he doesn't?"

I didn't answer right away. Instead, I stared at the fading sunset, wondering if love could survive in a space where commitment couldn't take root.

Later that night, my phone buzzed.

Jackson: *Hey, you up?*

I stared at the message for longer than I should have. It wasn't unusual for him to text late, but now, every interaction felt like another piece of a puzzle I wasn't sure I wanted to complete.

Me: *Yeah. What's up?*

His reply came quickly.

Jackson: *Just thinking about you.*

My breath hitched, fingers hovering over the keyboard.

I could say *me too*. I could say *I miss you*. But instead, I typed something different.

Me: *What are we doing, Jackson?*

This time, the reply didn't come as fast.

Minutes passed, and I imagined him staring at his phone, trying to find the right words. Or maybe, trying to decide if there were any words at all.

Finally—

Jackson: *I don't know.*

I squeezed my eyes shut, letting the weight of those three words settle over me.

Because deep down, I already knew.

I just didn't want to admit it.

Chapter 18

"Everyone has a right to be here and grieve, even those of you who knew did my boy wrong." I glanced at the floor. I never did him wrong- he did me wrong!

Jackson's uncertainty felt like a slow unraveling, pulling at the threads of something I wasn't ready to lose. And yet, when he called the next morning, asking me to come visit, I didn't hesitate.

I packed my bags within the hour.

The drive felt different this time- less like an adventure, more like a desperate attempt to hold onto something slipping through my fingers. My stomach twisted with every passing mile, my thoughts circling the same question: *If I just give him more, will he finally want me the way I want him?*

By the time I arrived, the air between us was light, easy, like nothing had ever been wrong. Jackson greeted me with his usual grin, pulling me into his arms, pressing a kiss against my temple like he'd missed me more than he could say. And for a moment, I let myself believe it.

We spent the first night wrapped up in the familiarity of each other, laughing, making music, and letting the world outside fade into something distant. But the next morning, things shifted.

"Let's go out," Jackson said, stretching lazily beside me. "I want to do something fun."

"Like what?" I asked, brushing sleep from my eyes.

He smirked. "Shopping."

I hesitated. "I don't know, Jackson. I've been trying to save."

"Come on, Jules," he coaxed, nudging me with his shoulder. "It's been forever since we went out and just *had fun*."

His voice was easy, persuasive, a carefully crafted invitation that made it sound like something harmless. Like something he needed.

And just like that, I caved.

The first store was harmless. He grabbed a couple of things- some new hoodies, a pair of sneakers- but as the day stretched on, the shopping spree grew into something bigger. Each store we entered, he found something else he *needed*, something that he just *had to have*.

"Babe, these look sick, right?" he said, holding up a pair of designer sunglasses, the price tag flashing a number that made my stomach twist. "I can see myself rocking these."

I forced a smile. "They're nice."

He slipped them on, grinning at his reflection in the mirror before turning to me, eyes playful but expectant. "Think you could cover this one? Just until I get paid next week."

I hesitated, my fingers tightening around my wallet. "Yeah. Sure."

I swiped my card. Again. And again.

It wasn't just the sunglasses. It was the jacket, the cologne, the expensive sneakers he swore would "last forever." Every time, he looked at me with those dark eyes, filled with charm and unspoken expectations, and I convinced myself that *this* would be enough. That if I just gave him more, he'd finally see that I was worth keeping.

By the time the day was over, my bank account was nearly drained, my stomach twisted in knots that had nothing to do with hunger.

"You're amazing, you know that?" Jackson grinned, swinging a bag over his shoulder as we stepped out into the crisp afternoon air. "Seriously, I don't know what I'd do without you."

My chest tightened. "You don't have to keep saying that."

"I mean it." He looped an arm around my shoulders, pressing a kiss to my temple. "Not just because of this. You're just... you're everything."

Everything.

It should have felt like enough.

But the weight of my nearly empty bank account and the hollow feeling in my chest told me otherwise.

As we drove back to his place, the car packed with bags, I stared out the window, my fingers gripping my thighs.

Maybe if I just kept giving, he'd finally realize what I already knew.

That I was the only one willing to do *anything* to make this work.

That I was the only one *trying*.

Chapter 19

I looked back up and she was staring right at me, I looked away and let a tear fall. As if I didn't feel bad enough.

The bags sat in the backseat, a silent reminder of everything I had given him that day. My bank account was nearly empty, and yet, Jackson was as carefree as ever, drumming his fingers against the steering wheel to the beat of the music playing low on the radio.

"Today was fun, huh?" he said, glancing at me with that easy smile, the one that had always made me feel like I belonged.

I nodded, forcing a smile of my own. "Yeah, it was."

But inside, I felt sick.

Jackson had gotten everything he wanted, and I had paid for it. Again. And still, I wasn't sure if I had bought his love or just rented his attention for another night.

I stole a glance at him, at the way his fingers tapped absentmindedly on his leg, at the way his new jacket fit snugly over his frame. It looked good on him. Everything always looked good on him.

"Hey," he said suddenly, his voice soft. "You okay?"

I swallowed, nodding too quickly. "Yeah. Just tired."

Jackson reached over, his fingers skimming over my thigh before squeezing lightly. "Don't stress about the money, okay? I'll pay you back."

We both knew that wasn't true.

I laughed weakly, looking out the window. "I know."

That night, Jackson wanted to celebrate.

"We should go out," he said, stretching lazily across the couch. "Have a drink, let loose a little."

I hesitated. My funds were already stretched thin, and the thought of spending more made my stomach churn. But I could already see it in his eyes- the slight gleam, the quiet expectation. Jackson was the kind of person who got what he wanted.

And I was the kind of person who gave it to him.

"Alright," I said. "Let's go."

The bar was crowded, dimly lit, filled with the low hum of conversation and clinking glasses. Jackson ordered without hesitation, and when the bartender slid the drinks across the counter, he barely made a move for his wallet.

I paid.

Again.

The first drink went down too easily, numbing the weight in my chest. The second was stronger, blurring the sharp edges of my doubt. By the third, I had stopped counting.

"You're too good to me, Jules," Jackson murmured, his arm slung around my shoulders as he leaned in, his lips grazing my ear. "I don't deserve you."

I wanted to believe that was true. I wanted to believe that if I kept giving, if I kept proving how much I loved him, eventually, he'd realize he loved me just as much.

"You deserve everything," I whispered back, my fingers tightening around my glass.

His lips brushed my temple, his breath warm against my skin. "That's why I've got you, huh?"

I smiled, but it didn't quite reach my eyes.

Love shouldn't have to be bought. But that's exactly what I was doing.

When we got back to his place, I could barely keep my eyes open. Jackson, however, was wide awake, flipping through channels like the world wasn't caving in around me.

"You're quiet tonight," he noted, glancing at me. "You sure you're okay?"

I hesitated. "Yeah. Just thinking."

Jackson stretched, exhaling a satisfied sigh. "Don't overthink it, babe. It's just money. We had fun, right?"

I nodded because that's what he wanted to hear.

But as I lay there in the dark later that night, my heart pounding against my ribcage, I wondered how much more of myself I could give before there was nothing left to offer.

How much more I could spend before I was empty in every possible way.

Chapter 20

Ceci gripped my arm when my body went rigid. His mom stepped down from the podium and there was another moment of silence-waiting for the next person to stand. I fought internally, until a girl around my age, stood up.

The morning after felt like a slow descent into reality. The shopping bags were still there, stacked in the corner of Jackson's apartment, a quiet reminder of everything I had given. Everything I had lost. My savings had taken a hit, but worse than that, my pride had too.

Jackson stretched beside me, rubbing the sleep from his eyes. "You're up early."

I forced a small smile. "Couldn't sleep."

He propped himself up on his elbow, watching me for a moment before reaching out to tuck a stray strand of hair behind my ear. "Last night was fun, though, right?"

I hesitated, then nodded. "Yeah. It was."

The truth sat heavy on my tongue. I wasn't sure if fun was the right word.

Jackson kissed my forehead before rolling out of bed, leaving me alone with my thoughts. I pulled the blankets tighter around me, staring at the ceiling.

I had done so much for him. Paid for things he wanted. Given him my time, my love, my everything. So why did it still feel like I was waiting for him to choose me?

By the afternoon, I was sitting on the couch, scrolling through my banking app, my stomach twisting at the sight of my balance. I had spent too much. Rent was due soon. My next paycheck wouldn't cover everything.

Jackson strolled in, a satisfied grin on his face. "Hey, what do you think about hitting that new steakhouse downtown tonight? My buddy said it's unreal."

I looked up at him, my fingers tightening around my phone. "Jackson... I can't keep paying for everything."

He blinked, caught off guard. "I told you I'd pay you back."

"When?" The question slipped out before I could stop it, sharper than I had intended. "Because I have bills piling up that I don't see myself getting out of."

His easygoing expression faltered for just a moment before he recovered. "Jules, come on. You know I've been trying to figure things out. Work's been slow. I thought you understood that."

I exhaled, trying to keep my voice steady. "I do understand. But that doesn't change the fact that I'm the one covering everything. It's not just *your* money, Jackson. It's mine. And I don't have a safety net."

Silence stretched between us. His jaw tensed, I saw something in his expression that unsettled me- not anger, not even guilt. Just... indifference.

"So, what? You regret helping me?" he asked, tilting his head slightly. "Because that's what it sounds like."

I swallowed hard. "That's not what I'm saying. But I need to know this isn't one-sided. That I'm not just- "

"Not just what?" Jackson scoffed. "Throwing your money away?"

I flinched.

For a split second, something flickered in his eyes- an emotion I couldn't quite place. Then, just as quickly as it came, it was gone.

He sighed, running a hand through his hair. "Look, I get it. You're stressed. If you need space, just say that. But don't make it seem like I'm using you."

Wasn't he?

The thought struck me harder than I expected, and suddenly, I wasn't sure if I wanted to be here anymore.

I stood up, grabbing my jacket. "I'm going for a drive."

Jackson watched me, his expression unreadable. "Jules."

I hesitated, waiting. Waiting for him to say something- anything- that would make this feel like it wasn't crumbling.

I walked out without another word, the weight of everything I had been holding in pressing down on my chest like a stone.

I drove aimlessly for an hour, letting the music drown out the thoughts swirling in my head. The sun was beginning to set when I finally pulled into a parking lot overlooking the city, my hands gripping the steering wheel so tightly my knuckles ached.

My phone buzzed. I expected it to be Jackson, but it wasn't.

Ceci: *You okay?*

My fingers hovered over the keyboard. No, I wasn't okay. I was exhausted. I was hurt. And worst of all, I was starting to wonder if Jackson ever really loved me, or if I had just been convenient.

I typed back a simple reply.

Me: *I don't know.*

I let myself feel what I had been avoiding all along:

Maybe love wasn't supposed to feel this way.

Chapter 21

She introduced herself as Holly, a friend. "I knew he was struggling, I just didn't know how bad it was."

The drive back to Jackson's apartment felt longer than it should have. The sunset cast long shadows over the road, stretching across the asphalt like silent warnings I didn't want to acknowledge. I had needed that hour away, needed the time to breathe, but it hadn't solved anything. It hadn't changed the sinking feeling in my stomach that told me something between us was shifting, slipping, breaking.

When I parked outside his complex, I didn't move right away. My hands stayed wrapped around the steering wheel, my pulse steady but slow, heavy with indecision. If I walked back inside, if I let this slide again, what did that say about me?

What did that say about *us*?

I finally forced myself out of the car, my chest tightening as I climbed the stairs. The door was unlocked when I twisted the handle, and I stepped inside to find Jackson lounging on the couch, his phone in one hand, a beer in the other.

He barely glanced up. "Hey. You good now?"

A strange sort of numbness spread through me. "Yeah."

He nodded like that was enough, like everything was fine, and went back to whatever held his attention on his phone. I stared at him, at the easy way he dismissed my absence, at the way he acted like I hadn't walked out on him an hour ago with my heart in my throat.

I wanted him to look at me. *Really* look at me. To see what was unraveling between us and care enough to fix it.

Instead, he took another sip of his beer. "You eat yet?"

I shook my head. "No."

He finally put his phone down, stretching out like this was any other night. "You wanna order something? Or are we still in 'I can't pay for everything' mode?"

The words landed like a slap, and I stiffened.

"Wow," I murmured, crossing my arms. "That's how you want to play this?"

Jackson sighed, rubbing a hand over his face. "Jules, come on. I was joking."

"Were you?" I shot back. "Because it didn't sound like a joke."

His jaw clenched for a second before he shook his head, exhaling through his nose. "Look, I get it. You're feeling unappreciated or whatever. But you are appreciated, I am so grateful and thankful for you. I never pretended to have it all together. I thought you *got* that."

I stared at him, the weight of his words pressing down on my chest. "I do get it, Jackson. I've always gotten it. But *understanding* your situation doesn't mean I have to *carry* it for you."

His expression flickered, like he wasn't sure if he should be angry or guilty. "So what, you want me to feel bad? You want me to say some magic words to make you feel better about spending money on me?"

I swallowed, my throat burning. "I want to feel like I matter beyond what I can give you."

Silence settled between us, thick and suffocating. I saw it clearly- *he was never going to give me what I needed.* Not because he couldn't, but because he wouldn't.

I should have left right then. I should have picked up my bag and walked out without looking back. But instead, I sat down across from him, the weight of exhaustion sinking into my bones.

"I love you, Jackson." My voice was quieter than I intended, but steady. Honest. "But I can't be the only one fighting for this."

His fingers tapped against the beer bottle, his eyes locked on the label like it held an answer he couldn't give me. When he finally looked up, his expression was unreadable.

"I love you too, Jules. But I don't know if that's enough."

The words shattered something inside me.

I nodded, more to myself than to him. "Yeah. I don't know if it is either."

He didn't stop me when I got up. He didn't reach for me when I walked toward the door. And when I stepped outside into the cold night air, my heart splintering inside my chest, I realized something I should have known all along.

Loving someone isn't the same as being loved the right way.

Chapter 22

"I loved him. I loved him with everything in me. He was my soulmate." I could feel Ceci's breathing quicken as she squeezed my arm tighter. I glanced at her and back to Holly. "I was the one that found him."

I threw myself back into school and work with an intensity that felt almost desperate. The distractions helped. Between lectures, assignments, and back-to-back shifts at the brewery, I didn't have much time to sit with the hollow ache in my chest.

Ceci noticed the change first. "You're pushing yourself too hard," she said one evening as I wiped down the bar. "When was the last time you actually did something for *you*?"

I forced a smile. "This is for me. Keeping busy is good."

She raised a skeptical eyebrow but didn't press further.

The truth was, I needed the chaos. I needed the long hours, the studying, the exhaustion. Because the alternative was lying awake at night, replaying every moment with Jackson, wondering if I had made a mistake.

Then one night, *he* walked in.

At first, I barely noticed him. The bar was packed, and I was too busy filling drink orders to pay much attention. But then he slid into a seat near the end of the counter, and when I finally glanced up, his eyes locked onto mine with quiet curiosity.

Tall. Dark-haired. A little rough around the edges but effortlessly put together. He had the kind of presence that made people look twice. And right now, he was looking at *me*.

"You always work this hard?" His voice was smooth, carrying just the right amount of teasing.

I smirked, shaking my head as I slid a beer across the counter. "Only when I have to."

He took a sip, his gaze never leaving mine. "What's your name?"

I hesitated for only a second. "Juliette."

A slow smile spread across his lips. "Nice to meet you, Juliette. I'm Adrian."

Adrian.

The name settled into my mind, unfamiliar but intriguing.

I should have walked away. I should have kept my distance. But something about the way he watched me- attentive, interested, without expectation- felt *different*.

So when he said, "You ever take a break?" I surprised myself by saying, "Not often. But maybe I should."

I let myself wonder what it would be like to be wanted without having to *prove* my worth first.

Chapter 23

"I tried everything to keep him alive, I want you to know that. I did everything." Holly was shaking in sobs so hard she was stuttering over her words. Who was this girl? I gave a raised brow expression to Ceci, she shrugged her shoulders.

I had spent so long equating love with sacrifice that I barely recognized what it felt like to simply be wanted- without conditions, without obligation. Jackson had taught me that love was something I had to earn, that affection came with a price tag, whether emotional or financial. But Adrian... Adrian was different.

I first noticed him as a regular at the bar, one of those faces I learned to recognize in the crowd. He never demanded attention, never tried too hard to be noticed. But there was a quiet confidence about him, something unspoken that made me curious.

At first, our conversations were small, nothing more than casual banter while I poured drinks. But he started lingering, waiting until the rush died down to talk to me, asking about things that had nothing to do with work. He wasn't prying- just interested. In me.

One night, as I was wiping down the counter, he leaned in slightly. "You always work this hard?"

I smirked, tucking a strand of hair behind my ear. "Only when I have to."

"That doesn't sound like much fun."

I shrugged. "Fun's a luxury."

He studied me for a moment before nodding. "I get that. Still, seems like you could use a little bit of it."

I raised an eyebrow. "And let me guess- you're offering?"

His lips curled into a slow grin. "Maybe."

I laughed softly, shaking my head. "I'll think about it."

Jackson noticed the change before I even realized I had shifted.

"You've been different lately," he said one night when I finally answered his call.

I was sitting in my car after a long shift, debating whether or not to respond at all. "Different how?"

There was a long pause. "I don't know. Busier. Harder to reach."

I frowned, gripping the steering wheel tighter. "I've always been busy, Jackson."

"Not like this." His voice carried something I couldn't quite place- something between suspicion and irritation. "You seeing someone?"

The question caught me off guard. I hadn't done anything wrong. I wasn't his to question. Still, something inside me twisted.

"Why do you care?" I asked, my voice even.

Jackson scoffed. "I don't. Just wondering."

But I could hear it- the way his voice tensed ever so slightly, the way he exhaled a little too sharply. He cared.

For months, I had been the one waiting, the one chasing, the one trying to prove I was enough. But now, the dynamic had shifted.

And Jackson didn't like it.

A few nights later, Adrian asked again. This time, it wasn't just passing conversation.

He slid into his usual seat at the bar, watching as I moved behind the counter. "So, what's the verdict?"

I smirked, pouring a drink for another customer. "On what?"

"On me." He leaned forward slightly, resting his elbows on the counter. "You coming to dinner with me or what?"

I rolled my eyes, but there was no denying the warmth spreading through my chest. "You're persistent."

"I am," he admitted. "And I think you like it."

I did.

And so, I surprised myself when I said, "Alright. One dinner."

Adrian grinned. "Now we're talking."

As he left that night, a strange sensation settled in my chest. It wasn't love. It wasn't even close. But it was something new. Something light. Something that didn't make me feel like I had to prove my worth just to be wanted.

And maybe, for now, that was enough.

Chapter 24

I quickly pulled up my phone and did a quick Insta search of her. There she was, in his followers list. I tapped on her profile and scrolled, sunsets, bikini pictures, and a clean girl aesthetic. She wasn't his type. But there, her last posted picture, was a photo of her and him, a eulogy to their relationship as friends.

I hadn't been on a real date in what felt like years. Every outing with Jackson had come with an underlying expectation- either I was paying, or I was proving something. This felt different.

The night of my dinner with Adrian, Ceci sat on the edge of my bed, watching as I sifted through my closet. "You nervous?"

I exhaled, pulling out a simple black dress. "I don't know. Maybe? I don't even know why I said yes."

Ceci smirked. "Because he's hot and pays attention to you?"

I rolled my eyes but didn't argue. Instead, I pulled the dress over my frame and turned to the mirror. It wasn't overly fancy, but it was a step up from my usual attire. When was the last time I dressed up for myself? Not for a night out I was dragged into. Not to keep up appearances. Just... because?

Ceci studied my reflection and nodded. "You look good, Jules. Really good."

I offered a small smile. "Thanks."

Adrian picked me up right on time, arriving in a sleek but not overly flashy car. When I slid into the passenger seat, I caught the scent of his cologne- clean, subtle, effortless.

"You look incredible," he said, his voice smooth, as he pulled away from my apartment. "I was starting to think you might stand me up."

I smirked. "I thought about it."

He let out a low chuckle. "Honest. I like that."

I studied him as he drove, the way his fingers drummed absently against the steering wheel, his jaw sharp in the low streetlights. He wasn't just attractive- he carried himself with a kind of quiet assurance, like a man who knew exactly what he wanted and wasn't afraid of it.

It was new.

And I liked new.

The restaurant Adrian chose was perfect- nice but not over-the-top, intimate but not suffocating. He pulled out my chair before sitting across from me, his gaze unwavering.

"So," he said, picking up the menu. "Tell me something real about you. No surface-level stuff."

I raised an eyebrow. "That's a strong opener."

"I don't do small talk. I'd rather get to the good stuff."

I hesitated, then leaned back. "Okay. I used to think love was something you had to earn. That if you just did enough, gave enough, you'd get it in return. But now, I think maybe it's the other way around. The right person doesn't make you prove anything."

Adrian held my gaze, something flickering in his expression. "That's real."

I exhaled, feeling a strange sense of relief. "Your turn."

He smirked slightly, setting the menu down. "I used to think life had to be planned out perfectly. That if you weren't on a set path, you were wasting time. But now, I think maybe life is just a series of things you never saw coming. And you either roll with it or let it drown you."

I swallowed. "And which are you?"

He tilted his head. "I guess that depends on the day. Tonight? I'm rolling with it."

I didn't expect the date to feel so easy. I didn't expect the conversation to flow, for me to laugh as much as I did. But it did, and I did. And when he walked me back to my door at the end of the night, I found myself standing a little closer than I needed to.

"I had a good time," I said softly.

Adrian smiled, his eyes searching mine. "Me too."

There was a moment- one of those charged seconds where the air thickens, where the decision is right there, waiting to be made.

I had always been the one to reach, to chase, to hope for more than was offered. But tonight, I let him decide.

Adrian leaned in, his lips brushing softly against mine. It wasn't demanding, wasn't urgent- it was just there, real and present. When he pulled back, his thumb traced my cheek for the briefest second before he stepped away.

"I'll see you soon?" he asked.

I nodded. "Yeah."

He gave me one last smile before turning and walking away.

I closed the door behind me, exhaling slowly, my fingers pressing against my lips.

I wasn't overanalyzing. Wasn't questioning.

I just felt.

Chapter 25

I scrolled further, and the deeper I went, the more unsettling it became. Their friendship- if that's what it was- had been more than casual. Late-night car rides, drinks at dimly lit bars, pictures with captions that, in hindsight, felt intimate. There were candids of him, ones that I had never seen before, ones where he looked *happy* genuinely happy, not the forced kind of smile he had given me in the later years of our relationship.

The morning after my date with Adrian, I woke with an unfamiliar feeling- guilt. It sat heavy in my chest, dull and persistent, overshadowing the warmth of Adrian's lips on mine, the easy laughter we had shared.

Because the truth was, my heart was still tangled up in Jackson.

I moved through my morning in a daze, trying to push away the conflicting emotions that kept pressing in. By noon, I was back at the brewery, apron tied around my waist, running on autopilot. The lull between the lunch and evening rush gave me a rare moment of quiet, and I took the opportunity to check my phone.

Adrian: I had a great time last night.

A small smile tugged at my lips, but it didn't reach my eyes. I hesitated before typing back.

Me: Me too.

Simple. Easy. Safe. But the weight in my chest didn't ease.

Ceci's voice cut through my thoughts. "That better be Adrian."

I looked up to find my best friend leaning against the counter, arms crossed. "And if it is?"

Ceci smirked. "Then I'm happy for you. You deserve someone who looks at you like you matter."

I forced a chuckle, but inside, I felt like a fraud. Adrian did look at me like I mattered, but Jackson was the one who still had my heart- even when he didn't deserve it.

Before I could respond, the bell above the door chimed. I turned, expecting another customer, but instead, my stomach clenched at the sight of him.

Jackson.

He stepped inside like he belonged there, like he still had some kind of claim to my space. He looked the same- messy dark curls, easy confidence, the same tired charm that had once made me feel invincible. But tonight, all I felt was uncertainty.

His eyes found mine instantly, and something flickered behind them. "Hey, Jules."

My fingers tightened around the towel in my hand. "Jackson."

Ceci, to her credit, didn't say anything. But I could feel her presence at my side, solid and unwavering.

Jackson ran a hand through his hair, glancing around. "Didn't know if you'd still be working here."

"Still paying my bills, so yeah." I kept my tone neutral, unwilling to give him any opening to think this conversation was something I wanted.

He hesitated, shifting his weight. "You been good?"

I blinked. Was he serious?

"You don't get to ask me that," I said, voice steady but firm. "Not after everything."

His jaw tensed. "I know I messed up."

Understatement of the year.

He exhaled heavily, looking down before meeting my gaze again. "I've been thinking about what you said before you left. About how love isn't enough. And you were right."

My throat tightened. Hearing him say it, hearing him acknowledge what I had known all along, should have made me feel justified. Instead, it just made my chest ache.

"I paid you back," he added, pulling his phone from his pocket. "Just sent it through. I know it's late, but... it's something."

A notification buzzed on my phone. I glanced down- a transfer. More than I expected.

The weight in my chest lightened, but it didn't change the one thing that mattered most.

Jackson took a breath. "I don't want you to hate me, Jules."

I swallowed hard. "I don't hate you."

His eyes searched mine. "But?"

My hands curled into fists at my sides. "But I still love you. And I hate myself for it."

Jackson's expression cracked, raw emotion flashing across his face. He took a half-step forward before stopping himself, running a hand through his hair. "Jules..."

I shook my head quickly, stopping him before he could say something that would only break me further. "I can't do this, Jackson. I can't be the only one who ever fights for us. I love you, but I won't keep setting myself on fire just to keep you warm."

Silence stretched between us, thick and suffocating. Jackson looked like he wanted to say something- maybe everything I had been waiting to hear- but the words never came.

I took a step back. "Goodbye, Jackson."

I turned, but before I could take another step, Jackson was there, grabbing my wrist, spinning me back toward him.

"No," he breathed. His grip was firm but not forceful, his dark eyes blazing with something desperate. "I'm not letting you walk away like this."

I barely had time to process his words before his lips crashed against mine.

The restaurant went silent. The weight of everyone watching should have made me self-conscious, should have made me pull away. But the second Jackson's mouth met mine, everything else faded. It wasn't just a kiss. It was a declaration. A refusal. A promise.

His hands slid to cup my face, his fingers trembling against my skin. "I love you, Juliette.

And I don't care how much I've messed up- I can't let you go. I won't."

I pulled back just enough to breathe, my forehead pressed against his. "Jackson..."

"Tell me you don't feel this," he whispered, his voice cracking. "Tell me you don't love me, and I'll let you go."

My heart slammed against my ribs. I couldn't lie to him. Not about this.

Tears stung my eyes as I whispered, "I do."

Jackson exhaled sharply, his arms wrapping around me like he was afraid I'd slip away. "Then don't leave. Not yet."

I let out a shaky breath, my fingers curling into his jacket. I wasn't ready to forgive everything, wasn't ready to forget the ways he had hurt me.

But right now, walking away felt impossible.

Chapter 26

I exhaled slowly, my fingers tightening around my phone. Who *was* she to him? A friend, or something more? Had she been there all along, in the background of my life with him, loving him while I was desperately trying to hold together the pieces of a broken relationship?

Holly wiped her tears with the sleeve of her sweater, sniffling. "I just- I just wanted you to know he wasn't alone. He had people who *really* loved him."

Something in her tone twisted in my chest. *People who really loved him.* As if I hadn't. As if my love had been *less* than hers.

Ceci shifted beside me, her posture stiff, as if she could sense the same undercurrent in Holly's words. "Yeah, well," Ceci muttered under her breath, just loud enough for me to hear. "Didn't seem to stop him from ruining lives."

The entire brewery had gone silent. I could feel the weight of dozens of eyes on me, on us, as Jackson held me close like he had no intention of letting go. His breath was warm against my cheek, his heartbeat rapid beneath my hands, as if he had been running toward this moment for as long as I had been running from it.

My mind screamed at me to pull away, to put distance between us before I fell too hard—before I forgot all the reasons I left in the first place.

But my body refused to move.

Jackson's fingers trembled slightly against my jaw, his touch softer now, gentler.

"Come outside with me," he murmured. "Just for a minute."

I hesitated, torn between logic and emotion. But the desperation in his eyes- the sheer need in his voice- shattered my defenses.

Without a word, I let him take my hand and lead me out the front door.

The night air was crisp, biting against my flushed skin. The second we stepped outside, Jackson exhaled sharply, like he had been holding his breath since the moment he saw me.

I crossed my arms, trying to create some semblance of space between us. "You can't just do that, Jackson. You can't just kiss me like- like none of it happened."

His gaze darkened. "None of it happened? Jules, everything happened. And I messed up. I know that. But don't pretend like what just happened in there wasn't real."

I swallowed hard, my pulse still racing. "It's not about whether it was real. It's about whether it changes anything."

Jackson took a step closer, eyes searching mine. "It changes everything."

"How?" I challenged. "You think one kiss fixes this? Fixes us?"

His jaw tightened. "No. But it proves that you're still here. That we still exist. And that means there's still something worth saving."

My breath hitched, and I hated how much I wanted to believe him. "Jackson..."

"Please, just listen to me," he cut in, his voice raw. "I know I hurt you. I know I made you feel like you were the only one fighting for us, and that's on me. But losing you? It made me realize what I've always known but was too much of a coward to admit."

My fingers curled into fists at my sides. "And what's that?"

He stepped in close, close enough that I could see the flicker of emotion in his deep brown eyes. "That I've never loved anyone the way I love you. That I don't want to love anyone else. That I should have fought for you before, and I won't make that mistake again."

Tears burned at the edges of my vision, my heart screaming at me to let go of all the pain, to give in to the part of me that still wanted him- needed him.

But love had never been the problem. It was everything else.

I took a slow, shuddering breath. "Loving me isn't enough, Jackson. You have to be better. I can't go back to the way things were."

"Then don't." His voice was firm now, steady. "We start over. We do it right this time."

I shook my head. "It's not that simple."

"Maybe not," he admitted. "But I don't care how long it takes, Jules. I just need to know that you'll let me try."

Silence stretched between us, heavy and uncertain. The past loomed in the air around us, threatening to pull us under.

But standing here, in the quiet of the night, Jackson was still the only thing that made me feel like home.

And that scared me more than anything.

I exhaled slowly. "I don't have an answer for you right now."

Jackson nodded, swallowing hard. "Then don't give me one. Just... don't shut me out."

I hesitated, then gave the smallest nod. It wasn't a yes, but it wasn't a no either.

Jackson reached for my hand, lacing his fingers through mine. "Can I come home with you tonight? Just to talk. Just to be us for a little while. No pressure."

My breath caught. "Jackson..."

"Please." His voice was barely above a whisper. "I just want to hold you. I don't know how to sleep without you anymore."

The ache in my chest was unbearable. Because I knew exactly what he meant.

Finally, I whispered, "Okay."

Jackson's shoulders sagged in relief as he gently squeezed my hand, as if afraid I'd disappear if he let go.

And as we walked toward his car, I knew I was standing at the edge of something dangerous. Something uncertain.

Because letting Jackson back in was a risk. A chance at something real- or another disaster waiting to happen.

Yet, I didn't know if I cared.

Chapter 27

Holly didn't seem to hear her. Or maybe she did and didn't care. Instead, she sniffled again, adjusting the strap of her purse, her eyes searching mine like she was waiting for something- for me to validate her pain, to acknowledge that she had been just as much a part of his life as I had. But I couldn't.

I couldn't give her that.

Because standing there, looking at her, all I felt was a strange, quiet kind of anger. Not at her, not entirely. But at the realization that he had *never* truly been mine- not the way I had thought, not the way I had spent years convincing myself he was.

And maybe, in the end, that was what hurt the most.

The ride back to my apartment was quiet, but it wasn't uncomfortable. Jackson's hand rested on the center console, his fingers brushing against mine as if testing the waters, seeing if I'd pull away. I didn't.

The city lights blurred past the windshield, illuminating his face in flickering intervals. He looked different in this moment—calmer, but restless, like he was holding back words he didn't know how to say.

I stared out the window, trying to steady myself. The entire night had felt surreal, from the way Jackson kissed me in front of everyone to the way I let him pull me back in so easily. Every part of me knew this wasn't smart.

But love had never been smart.

"What are you thinking?" Jackson's voice was soft, barely cutting through the hum of the car.

I turned my head slightly, studying him. "That this feels familiar."

He glanced at me, his expression unreadable. "Is that a bad thing?"

I exhaled. "I don't know yet."

He nodded, gripping the steering wheel tighter. "I meant what I said, Jules. I don't want to lose you. I know I can't change the past, but I-"

"Jackson," I interrupted gently. "Let's just get through tonight. No promises. No pressure. Just... us."

Something in his eyes flickered with relief. "Okay."

My apartment felt smaller with Jackson in it, but not in a bad way. He moved around the space like he still belonged there, but cautiously, as if afraid he'd disturb the fragile peace between us.

I set my bag on the counter and turned to him. "Do you want anything? Water? Tea?"

Jackson smirked. "Tea? You think I'm the kind of guy who drinks tea?"

I rolled my eyes but couldn't stop the small smile from tugging at my lips. "Water it is."

As I grabbed a glass, I heard him exhale behind me. "Feels weird being here."

I didn't turn around. "Because you didn't think you'd ever come visit?"

"Because I didn't deserve to be back."

I froze for just a second before slowly setting the glass down. When I finally turned to face him, he was leaning against the counter, his head tilted slightly, watching me.

"Then why are you?" I asked quietly.

Jackson's eyes darkened, but not in the way I was used to. There was no arrogance, no smug certainty. Just something raw. "Because I love you. Because I never stopped. Because every night I spent without you felt like a punishment I earned."

I swallowed hard. "Jackson, I don't want to fall back into something that's just going to break me all over again."

He took a slow step toward me. "Then let me prove to you that I won't let that happen."

"And what if you can't?" I whispered.

He reached out, fingers brushing against my wrist, hesitant but warm. "Then I'll spend the rest of my life trying."

My breath hitched, and for a moment, all the reasons I should walk away scattered like dust in the wind. Jackson had always had this effect on me- making me forget how much he had hurt me and remember only how much I had loved him.

I closed my eyes, shaking my head. "I'm scared."

His grip tightened slightly. "Me too."

I opened my eyes then, meeting his gaze. "Stay tonight. But just to sleep. Just to be here."

Jackson nodded without hesitation. "That's enough."

And as we curled up in bed hours later, our bodies close but our hearts still cautious, I realized something terrifying.

I had never stopped loving Jackson.

And I wasn't sure if I ever would.

Chapter 28

I let out a slow, shaky breath, and stood up. Ceci squeezed my arm one final time before I pushed off and walked between the rows of pews. Shaking with every breath, the closer I was to him. Dead, lifeless, cold.

I cleared my throat and started, "It wasn't easy to love him. It was hard, enduring, and painful. But I did it, too. I loved him, too, at one point."

"I never imagined my life without him. Whether as a partner, a friend, an acquaintance, or someone simply who used to be."

The morning came too soon.

I stirred before the sun had fully risen, the early light creeping through the blinds, casting soft shadows across the room. I could feel Jackson's steady breathing beside me, his arm draped loosely around my waist. It was a familiar warmth, one that sent a rush of nostalgia through me, threatening to pull me back into something I wasn't sure I should want.

For a long moment, I just lay there, letting myself feel it- him.

I had spent so many nights curled up alone, aching for this, for the way he held me like I was something precious. But now that I had it again, the weight of reality settled in my chest. Was this real? Or was I just feeding into the cycle all over again?

Jackson shifted, his fingers ghosting along my arm as he pulled me in closer. "You're awake."

His voice was thick with sleep, rough around the edges, and it sent an ache through my ribs.

"Mmhmm," I murmured, staring at the ceiling. "Barely."

Jackson pressed a lazy kiss against my shoulder. "Did you sleep okay?"

I hesitated. "I did."

He let out a soft sigh, his grip tightening just slightly. "Good. I didn't want to let go."

My throat tightened, but I forced a quiet laugh. "You snore, you know."

Jackson chuckled, his chest vibrating against my back. "Lies. I sleep like an angel."

I turned my head slightly, finally meeting his gaze. God, I had missed those eyes.

The moment stretched between us, unspoken words sitting heavy in the air. Jackson's fingers traced absent patterns against my hip, his expression shifting into something more serious.

"Jules," he said softly. "Talk to me. Where's your head at?"

I exhaled, rolling onto my back. "I don't know, Jackson. I don't know what this is."

He propped himself up on one elbow, watching me carefully. "This? This is me trying. This is me wanting you back. Wanting us back."

I bit my lip, blinking up at the ceiling. "But what if we just hurt each other again?"

Jackson reached for my hand, threading our fingers together. "Then we fight like hell to make sure we don't."

I turned my head toward him, searching for the sincerity in his face. And it was there- thank God, it was there.

"I don't want to be a mistake you make twice," I whispered.

Jackson's jaw tightened, his grip on my hand firm. "You were never a mistake, Jules. Losing you was. And if you let me, I'll spend every day proving that to you."

My heart twisted painfully. "You say that now, but what about when it gets hard? When life pulls us apart again?"

"Then I'll pull us back together," he said without hesitation. "Because I don't care how many times we break- I will always choose you. Always."

A tear slipped down my cheek, and Jackson was there, catching it with his thumb, brushing it away like it was something sacred.

I didn't have an answer. Not yet. Maybe not for a long time. But for now, I let him hold me. Let him kiss my forehead, let his warmth surround me.

Because maybe love wasn't about having all the answers.

Maybe it was just about choosing to try. Again and again.

Chapter 29

"At one point in my life, he was my best friend. I didn't think I would ever live without him. I am sure we all never thought we would be here, meeting under these circumstances."

The first few weeks back together were intoxicating. Jackson called and texted me constantly when we weren't together, filling the distance with words and reminders that I was always on his mind. When we visited each other, the world felt small again, like it had only ever been us.

But the distance was there. And distance was a thief.

I threw myself into school, determined to finish my degree by the end of the semester. Between studying, working shifts at the brewery, and trying to maintain a relationship with Jackson, the exhaustion crept in slowly, then all at once.

And then, there was Adrian.

I didn't mean for it to happen, but I waited to tell Adrian about Jackson. Maybe part of me wasn't ready for the high to wear off, for reality to settle in. Maybe part of me still wanted to keep Adrian around, just in case.

But Adrian wasn't stupid. He saw the way I hesitated now, the way I stopped lingering at his seat after my shifts, the way I looked over my shoulder as if checking to see if I was being watched.

One night, as I wiped down the bar, Adrian finally asked, "You back with him?"

My hands froze on the cloth. I didn't meet his eyes. "I don't know."

Adrian scoffed, shaking his head. "Yeah, you do."

I swallowed hard. "It's complicated."

"No, Jules," Adrian said, leaning forward. "It's simple. He's either changed, or he hasn't. He either treats you right, or he doesn't. And if you have to think about it this much, maybe you already have your answer."

My stomach twisted. "You don't know him."

"I know you," he shot back. "And I know you deserve better."

I looked away, pressing my lips together. "It's not that easy."

Adrian exhaled, shaking his head. "It is. You just don't want it to be."

I didn't answer. Because I didn't know how to.

Jackson sensed it before I ever said a word. The shift, the uncertainty. And the jealousy burned in him like an old wound reopening.

"Is there something going on with you and him?" he asked one night over the phone.

My breath caught. "Jackson..."

"Just tell me the truth."

I closed my eyes. "I saw him at work again and we talked."

Silence stretched between us before Jackson let out a quiet, bitter laugh. "And what? You needed to see if you still had options?"

My chest ached. "That's not fair."

"Neither is this distance," Jackson bit out. "Neither is knowing there's another guy right there while I'm stuck three hours away wondering if I'm wasting my time."

I felt something snap inside me. "Then don't waste it."

Jackson was quiet for a long time. When he finally spoke, his voice was soft but sharp. "Do you even want this?"

Tears burned my eyes. "Yes. But I don't know how to make it work."

Jackson inhaled deeply, steadying himself. "Now you finally understand where I was coming from. We'll figure it out. But we do it together."

That night, I made a decision.

If we were going to work, we had to be together. No more distance. No more in-between.

I opened my laptop and started looking at apartments. It was time to make a choice.

Chapter 30

"I knew a lot about him, things he kept from a lot of people. Things he kept deep inside. He was hurting more than we all could know."

The next week of my life became a blur of apartment listings, rental websites, budgeting spreadsheets, and endless comparisons of neighborhoods. Jackson was right- distance was killing us. If we wanted this to last, something had to change.

Jackson sent me listings too, each message coming with a hopeful, what do you think of this one? But nothing felt quite right yet.

I needed this next step to be more than just a solution to a problem. It had to be the beginning of something better.

"What about this one?" Ceci asked, leaning over my laptop as she scrolled through another listing. "It's not too far from your job, and the rent isn't awful."

I clicked through the photos, chewing my lip. "It's nice, but it's small. If Jackson moves in, we'd be on top of each other."

"I thought you liked that," Ceci teased, nudging me.

I rolled my eyes but smiled. "Not all the time."

Truthfully, I wasn't just looking for any apartment- I was looking for home. Somewhere Jackson wouldn't feel like he was just visiting, where we could wake up together without thinking about how many days we had left before one of us had to drive away.

The thought made my stomach twist with nerves. Were we really ready for this?

Jackson seemed to be. He called me every morning, texted me during my shifts, sent me voice memos when he knew I was too tired to type. He told me he missed me before I could say it first. And yet, part of me still hesitated.

"What if we move in together, and it doesn't work?" I asked quietly.

Ceci shut the laptop, leveling me with a look. "And what if it does?"

I sighed, rubbing my temples. "I just don't want to screw this up again."

"Jules, you're overthinking. You love him. He loves you. You've been together long-distance for months now, and you're still choosing each other. That means something."

It did. But it didn't erase the fear that had rooted itself inside me.

Later that night, I FaceTimed Jackson while curled up in bed, my laptop still open beside me. His face filled the screen, hair slightly tousled from running his hands through it.

"Any luck?" he asked, propping his phone up as he leaned back against his pillows.

I sighed. "A few places look decent. I just want to find something that feels... right."

Jackson's expression softened. "I get that."

We sat in silence for a moment before he shifted, voice quieter now. "Jules, are you sure you want this?"

My breath hitched. "What do you mean?"

"I mean, I don't want you to feel like you have to do this. I know this is a big step, and if you're not ready- "

"I want this, Jackson," I cut in, my voice firmer than I expected. "I just... I want to get it right this time."

Jackson nodded slowly. "We will."

I wanted to believe that. I really did.

"Hey, I have an idea," he said, his lips twitching into a small smile. "How about I come up this weekend, and we go look at places together? Make a real trip out of it."

I smiled. "You'd do that?"

"I'd do anything for you," he murmured. "You know that."

My heart swelled. Maybe, just maybe, this could work.

The weekend arrived faster than I expected. Jackson drove up on Friday afternoon, and by Saturday morning, we were sitting in a leasing office, flipping through paperwork on a potential apartment.

"This one has a lot of space," I said, glancing around the model unit. "And the kitchen is actually big enough for two people."

Jackson leaned against the counter, watching me. "You'd let me cook?"

I smirked. "No."

He laughed, pulling me into his arms. "You're impossible."

"And you love it."

His smile softened. "I do."

We toured two more places before grabbing lunch, sitting across from each other in a quiet café. I toyed with the edge of my napkin, nerves buzzing under my skin.

"This is really happening, isn't it?" I murmured.

Jackson reached across the table, squeezing my hand. "Yeah. It is."

Maybe this was the right step. Maybe we were finally getting it right.

But just as we were starting to feel steady, my phone rang.

I glanced at the screen, my stomach dropping at the caller ID.

It was a number I hadn't seen in a long time.

Frowning, I answered. "Hello?"

There was a pause, then a voice I barely recognized mumbled through the phone. "Juliette? I... I don't know how to say this, but- it's Cory."

My blood ran cold.

"What about him?" I asked, my voice barely above a whisper.

Another pause. Then the words that shattered everything.

"He's gone. He overdosed last night."

My breath left me in a rush, the world tilting beneath me.

Jackson sat up straighter. "Jules? What is it?"

I couldn't speak. Couldn't move. The sound of the café faded, replaced by the roaring in my ears.

Cory was dead.

And suddenly, I was right back where I started.

Chapter 31

"I respected him in life and in death and like everyone else, I hope he is in a better place." I felt a tear rolling down my face as I stepped back from the podium. Memories of our past flooding back the moment I catch a glance at his lifeless face.

A face I once held and kissed hundreds of times. A face I thought I love when I thought I knew what love was.

I barely registered Jackson's voice as he called my name. The walls of the café seemed to close in, the noise of clinking dishes and quiet conversations turning into nothing more than muffled background static. Cory was dead.

The words didn't feel real. They hung in the air, pressing against my chest like a vice, suffocating me with their weight.

"Jules." Jackson's hand found mine, grounding me when I felt like I might float away. "Talk to me. What happened?"

My fingers trembled as I gripped the phone tighter. "I- I have to go."

I didn't wait for Jackson's response before standing up, nearly knocking my chair over in the process. The room felt too bright, too sharp, and every step I took toward the exit felt disconnected from my body. Jackson was right behind me, his voice laced with concern, but I couldn't focus. Not yet. Not now.

Once outside, I pressed the phone back to my ear. "Who- who found him?"

The voice on the other end hesitated. "Some girl named Holly and his mom."

I closed my eyes. Of course. Cory's mother, the woman who had once adored me, who had hugged me like a daughter before our relationship imploded. Now she would have to bury her son. The thought sent a fresh wave of nausea through me, and I bent at the waist, bracing my hand against the rough brick wall.

Memories of Cory flooded my mind: the carefree laugh, the nights we spent under the stars talking about everything and nothing, the way he used to hold my hand like he was afraid to let go. And then the darker memories followed-the late-night phone calls when he was high, the accusations, the broken promises.

"When's the funeral?" I forced out.

"They're still making arrangements. I just... I thought you should know."

I swallowed the lump in my throat. "Thanks."

I ended the call before anything else could be said. My hand dropped to my side, the phone slipping from my grip and clattering onto the pavement.

A beat of silence stretched between me and Jackson before he spoke. "You're going, aren't you?"

I turned toward him, my vision blurring at the edges. "I have to."

Jackson's jaw tensed, his hands shoved deep into his jacket pockets. "You don't owe him anything, Jules."

But I did. I owed him the memories, the history, the love that once existed between us- even if it had turned to ruin. I owed myself the chance to say goodbye to the boy who had once meant everything to me.

"I know," I whispered. "But I have to go."

Jackson exhaled slowly, his eyes softening with understanding. He didn't try to talk me out of it again. Instead, he closed the distance between us, pulling me into his arms. The warmth of his embrace, the steady beat of his heart against my cheek, anchored me when everything else felt like it was unraveling.

"I'll come with you," he said softly.

"You don't have to."

"I know. But I'm not letting you do this alone."

Tears stung my eyes, and I buried my face in his chest, letting myself lean into his strength.

Chapter 32

The funeral was three days later, held in the same church where Cory's family had celebrated birthdays and holidays for years. I sat in the third row, my hands clenched in my lap, my entire body stiff with unspoken grief.

I wasn't sure how I was supposed to feel. Cory hadn't been a good man, not in the end. He had hurt me. He had cheated, manipulated, taken from me. But he had also been my first love, the boy I had once believed would be my forever.

Tears burned at the edges of my eyes, but I didn't let them fall. I simply listened to the hollow words of the priest, to the quiet sobs of Cory's mother, to the murmur of old friends whispering condolences. The memories played like a distant film reel in my mind: the laughter, the fights, the moments when I thought love alone could fix us.

And then, suddenly, it was over.

I stayed seated as people filtered out, my heart hammering in my chest. I could feel Jackson before I saw him, his presence steady, unwavering. When I finally turned, he was there, dressed in all black, waiting at the back of the church.

"Ready to go?" he asked softly.

The breath I had been holding finally escaped.

Jackson was here. He was real. He was alive.

The weight of the past loosened, just slightly, and I nodded. "Yeah. I'm ready."

As we stepped outside, the sun broke through the clouds, casting a warm glow on the church steps. The fresh air filled my lungs, but it didn't erase the heaviness that sat just beneath the surface.

I had spent so long mourning what was lost, what could never be again. But standing here, with Jackson by my side, I knew one thing for certain.

I didn't want to be lost In the meantime anymore.

CHAPTER 33

The drive back from the funeral was silent. I watched the world blur past through the window, my thoughts tangled between past and present. The ache in my chest wasn't for Cory himself but for what he had been- the boy I once loved, the boy who had loved me in his own twisted way before it all went wrong. The boy who had made me feel like forever was possible, only to rip it away piece by piece.

I traced a finger against the cool glass, watching as raindrops collected and slid down in jagged paths. The sky mirrored the heaviness pressing in on me- gray, heavy, unsettled. It felt fitting. Like the world itself was mourning something that had long since been lost.

Jackson's fingers tapped against the steering wheel, his knuckles tightening every time he glanced at me. He wanted to say something, I could feel it, but I wasn't sure if I had the energy to hear it yet.

Finally, he broke the silence. "Are you okay?"

I let out a slow breath. "I don't know."

Jackson nodded like he understood, because maybe he did. Maybe he saw the way grief wrapped itself around me, even if it wasn't the traditional kind. Maybe he knew that losing someone you had already lost long ago was still its own kind of pain.

"You want to talk about it?" he asked, his voice careful, measured.

"I don't think there's anything to say." I turned to look at him, really look at him. His jaw was set, his brows drawn together just slightly—concern woven into every inch of him. "I just need today to be over."

He didn't push. Instead, he reached for my hand, lacing his fingers through mine. "Then let's go home."

The word home sent a warmth through my chest. I didn't know if it was the right word yet, but with Jackson, it felt close enough.

Back at my apartment, exhaustion hit me in waves. I kicked off my heels, peeled off the black dress, and crawled under the blankets without another word. The funeral had drained me- physically, emotionally, in ways I hadn't been prepared for.

Jackson followed my lead, slipping into bed beside me, his body warm and solid against mine. He smelled like rain, like the faint remnants of his cologne, like comfort. He pulled the blankets over both of us, his arm wrapping around my waist, grounding me in ways I didn't know I needed.

"You still with me?" he murmured, pressing a kiss to my shoulder.

I let out a soft hum. "Barely."

He chuckled, but there was something heavier beneath it. "You're thinking too much."

"I can't help it."

I wasn't just thinking- I was unraveling. The funeral had stirred something inside me, a reminder of the past I had buried but never fully left behind. Seeing Holly there, sobbing like she had lost a piece of herself, had made me wonder—had Cory ever been capable of loving someone wholly? Or had he just been collecting pieces of different women, filling the void inside him with stolen affections?

Jackson was quiet for a long time before he finally said, "I know this wasn't easy for you. But I need you to know something."

I shifted to face him, my forehead resting against his. "What?"

"I'm not going anywhere." His voice was steady, unwavering. "You don't have to figure everything out right now. You don't have to know what happens next. But I'm here, Jules. And I'm staying."

My throat tightened. I wanted to believe him, wanted to let myself fall completely. But there was still that lingering voice in the back of my mind whispering that love had never been enough before. That promises had been made and broken before. That forever had always been temporary in my life.

"What if I break us again?" I whispered.

Jackson shook his head. "Then I'll put us back together. As many times as it takes."

A tear slipped down my cheek, but this time, it wasn't just grief- it was relief.

Jackson pulled me closer, his thumb brushing against my cheek, tracing the path of the tear. "You don't have to carry all of this alone. You never did."

I let out a shaky breath, pressing myself against him, letting the warmth of his body soothe the ache inside me. He was here. He wasn't leaving.

I pressed my lips to his, slow and lingering. "I love you."

Jackson smiled against my mouth. "I love you more."

Maybe that was enough. Maybe it always had been.

And maybe, just maybe, I could let myself believe it this time.

Chapter 34

Two weeks later, I stood in the middle of an empty apartment, the keys cold in my palm. The walls were bare, the floors freshly cleaned, the possibilities endless. The air smelled like fresh paint, and the echo of our footsteps filled the space as we moved through the rooms that would soon become our home.

"Are we really doing this?" I asked, turning to Jackson, who was leaning against the doorway with a smirk.

"I signed the lease, didn't I?" he teased, stepping inside and wrapping his arms around my waist. "This is happening."

I let out a breathless laugh, shaking my head. "It doesn't feel real."

Jackson lifted our intertwined hands and pressed a kiss to the back of mine. "It's real. And it's ours."

I looked around again, trying to picture our life here. The living room where we would cuddle on the couch. The kitchen where Jackson would insist on cooking even though he was a disaster with anything more complicated than eggs. The bedroom where I would fall asleep with his arms around me, knowing I was exactly where I was supposed to be.

"We need furniture," I mused, running a hand over the empty counter. "And a bed. And about a million other things."

Jackson grinned. "We'll get it. Piece by piece."

I turned to face him, my hands resting on his chest. "Are we really ready for this?"

His expression softened, his thumbs brushing against my hips. "We'll never know until we do it."

A part of me was still scared- scared of history repeating itself, scared of losing him again. But another part, the louder part, told me that this was different. That we had fought too hard to let this slip away.

Jackson leaned in, pressing a kiss to my forehead. "I love you, Jules. And I'm not running this time."

I let out a shaky breath, then smiled. "Then let's make this home."

We spent the rest of the afternoon unpacking the few boxes we had brought, making lists of what we still needed, and arguing over paint colors for the bedroom. It felt natural, easy, like we had been building toward this moment for longer than either of us realized.

As night fell, we collapsed onto a pile of blankets on the floor, our makeshift bed for the night. Jackson pulled me against him, his body warm, steady, and real.

"Tired?" he murmured against my hair.

I hummed. "Exhausted."

"Worth it, though?"

I smiled, pressing a kiss to his collarbone. "Completely."

I felt it- not just the love between us, but the peace of knowing I had finally stopped running.

I was exactly where I was meant to be.

I was home.

Chapter 35

The first few days in our new apartment were a mess of half-unpacked boxes, mismatched furniture, and the constant hum of possibility. The space still felt foreign, like we were living in a temporary bubble that hadn't yet solidified into something real.

I found myself pacing the living room, mentally arranging furniture that hadn't even been purchased yet. "I think the couch should go against that wall."

Jackson, lying on the floor with his hands behind his head, smirked. "You mean the couch we don't have?"

I rolled my eyes. "It's called planning."

He stretched lazily. "You plan, I execute. Works out."

I let out a breathless laugh before sitting down beside him. The hardwood was cold against my legs, but Jackson's warmth was close enough to chase away the chill. "Are we really doing this?" I asked, staring up at the ceiling.

Jackson turned his head to look at me, his expression soft. "We already did."

A quiet settled between us, the kind that felt like comfort instead of silence.

"I want this to work," I admitted. "I really do."

Jackson reached for my hand, threading our fingers together. "Then it will."

I wished I had his certainty, but for now, his belief in us was enough.

Our first grocery run together was chaotic in a way I hadn't expected. I had envisioned something efficient and methodical- list in hand, quick stops in each aisle. Instead, Jackson treated it like a field trip.

"We need this," he said, tossing a pack of gummy bears into the cart.

I frowned. "Since when do you eat gummy bears?"

"Since now."

I narrowed my eyes. "This isn't how adults shop."

"Then let's not be adults for a minute." He tossed in a box of toaster pastries with a grin. "Come on, Jules. Live a little."

I sighed, but the smile tugging at my lips betrayed me. "Fine. But we're sticking to the list for everything else."

Jackson saluted. "Yes, ma'am."

Despite myself, I laughed.

Nights were the easiest.

After the exhaustion of unpacking, settling, and trying to turn a hollow space into a home, there was something deeply soothing about curling up with Jackson in our barely furnished bedroom. Some nights, we talked until sleep stole our words; other nights, we let the quiet say everything we didn't need to.

One evening, as I lay against his chest, I murmured, "Do you think we'll still be like this in five years?"

Jackson ran his fingers lazily through my hair. "Like what?"

"Happy. Stable. Together."

He tilted my chin up, making me look at him. "I think as long as we keep choosing each other, yeah."

I swallowed, blinking up at him. "Even when it's hard?"

Jackson smiled. "Especially then."

I let out a slow breath, pressing my forehead against his. "I want to believe that."

"Then believe it."

I closed my eyes, letting his steady heartbeat lull me into rest.

CHAPTER 36

Things were good. Maybe too good.

I felt it creeping in- the slow, gnawing fear that happiness never lasted. That something would go wrong. That I'd wake up one day and realize this was all a beautiful illusion, doomed to shatter like everything before it.

Jackson had been steady, solid. He checked in when we were apart, helped build our home piece by piece, reminded me in quiet moments that he was here. That he wasn't leaving.

And still, I couldn't shake the unease.

"You're quiet today," Ceci observed as we sat at a coffee shop, laptops open but untouched. "What's going on?"

I exhaled, stirring my drink absentmindedly. "I don't know. Everything's just... a lot."

Ceci tilted her head. "A lot like good? Or a lot like bad?"

"Both."

She gave me a knowing look. "You think it's too good to be true."

I swallowed hard. "It always is."

Ceci sighed, leaning back. "You need to let yourself be happy, Jules. Jackson isn't Cory. And you're not the girl who let herself get walked over anymore."

I knew that. But knowing and believing were two different things.

That night, Jackson sensed something was wrong before I even spoke. He had a way of reading me, of picking up on the things I didn't say.

"Talk to me," he said, pulling me into his lap as we sat on the couch. "What's going on in that overthinking brain of yours?"

I hesitated, fingers playing with the hem of his shirt. "What if we're just setting ourselves up for another fall?"

Jackson's hands tightened on my waist. "Is that what you think?"

"I don't want to think that. But I'm scared. I don't know how to trust that this will last."

He studied me for a long moment before speaking. "Jules, I don't know what's going to happen five years from now. Hell, I don't know what's going to happen in five months. But I know that every single day, I wake up and choose you. And I'm going to keep choosing you. Even when you doubt. Even when it's hard."

My throat tightened. "What if I don't know how to believe that?"

Jackson cupped my face, his gaze steady. "Then I'll remind you. Every damn day."

A tear slipped down my cheek, and Jackson caught it with his thumb. "I love you," he whispered. "You don't have to be scared alone."

And just like that, the fear lost its grip, if only a little.

Maybe happiness didn't have to be temporary. Maybe love wasn't just borrowed time.

Maybe, this time, it was real.

Chapter 37

Graduation day arrived before I even had time to process it. The past few months had been a blur of late-night studying, long shifts at the brewery, and quiet moments with Jackson that grounded me when everything felt overwhelming.

But now, standing in my cap and gown, I felt the weight of it all.

"I can't believe you did it," Ceci said, bumping my shoulder. "Wait, no. I can believe it. You're kind of a badass."

I laughed, shaking my head. "I feel like I blinked and suddenly I'm here."

"That's how it works. One minute you're drowning in assignments, the next you're walking across a stage."

I took a deep breath. "It doesn't feel real."

"It's real, Jules. And you earned this."

Before I could respond, I heard my name- Jackson's voice cutting through the crowd.

I turned just in time to see him making his way toward me, pride shining in his eyes. He wrapped me in his arms, lifting me off the ground in a tight hug. "I am so proud of you."

I clung to him, the moment sinking into my bones. "Thank you for believing in me."

Jackson pulled back just enough to kiss my forehead. "Always."

The post-ceremony celebration was small but perfect. We sat at a cozy restaurant, me sandwiched between Jackson and Ceci, while laughter and conversation flowed effortlessly around the table. I let myself soak it all in- the warmth of the people I loved, the knowledge that I had accomplished something huge.

"So what's next?" Ceci asked, raising an eyebrow. "You're officially done with school. The world is yours."

I hesitated, then looked at Jackson. "I don't know yet. But I want to figure it out- we want to figure it out together."

Jackson squeezed my hand. "And we will."

Later that night, when it was just the two of us in our apartment, I curled up against Jackson's chest, listening to his steady breathing.

"I was so scared," I admitted. "For so long, I thought I was stuck in a cycle I'd never break. That I was always going to be running from something."

Jackson kissed the top of my head. "And now?"

I tilted my head up, meeting his gaze. "Now, I think I was always running toward something. Toward you. Toward this."

Jackson smiled, brushing a strand of hair from my face. "We're going to be okay, Jules."

As I drifted off to sleep in Jackson's arms, I realized something profound.

I had spent so much of my life waiting for things to fall apart.

But maybe, just maybe, things were finally falling into place.

Chapter 38

The first few weeks after graduation felt like stepping into the unknown. For the first time in years, there were no looming deadlines, no assignments hanging over my head, no tests to study for. The absence of structure was strange—freeing but terrifying.

Most mornings, I made coffee while Jackson slept in. Afternoons were spent scrolling through job postings I wasn't even sure I wanted. At night, I curled up beside him, wondering what came next.

"Are you feeling restless?" Jackson asked one evening as we sat on our small balcony, watching the city lights flicker against the sky.

I sighed, tucking my legs beneath me. "A little. I guess I just thought I'd have everything figured out by now."

Jackson smirked, taking a slow sip of his beer. "Jules, no one has everything figured out. We just pretend we do."

I laughed, shaking my head. "So what's your big plan, then?"

He set his beer down and reached for something in his pocket. At first, I didn't think much of it—not until he took a deep breath, turned toward me fully, and pulled out a small velvet box.

My breath caught in my throat. "Jackson..."

He opened the box, revealing a simple but beautiful ring. "I don't know what comes next," he admitted. "I don't have a perfect plan, and I sure as hell don't have all the answers. But what I do know is that every future I picture has you in it. So let's stop worrying about the unknown and build something real—together. Juliette Grace, will you marry me?"

My heart pounded in my chest, emotions crashing into me all at once. I hadn't expected this—not yet, maybe not ever—but as I looked at him, at the absolute certainty in his eyes, I realized something.

I didn't need a perfect plan. I just needed him.

A breathless laugh escaped me as I nodded. "Yes. Yes, Jackson, of course."

A grin spread across his face as he slipped the ring onto my finger. It fit perfectly, as if it had always belonged there. He leaned in, capturing my lips in a kiss, sealing the promise between us.

The following days blurred into a haze of wedding talks, job applications, and something neither of us had expected to consider so soon—buying a home.

"We could rent for a while," I reasoned, scrolling through listings on my laptop. "Just until we figure things out."

Jackson sat beside me, looking at a separate screen, his brow furrowed. "Or... we could just go for it. Buy a place. Start fresh."

I arched an eyebrow. "You're seriously thinking about buying?"

He shrugged. "Why not? If we're building a life together, we might as well have something that's ours. Something permanent."

My stomach flipped. The idea had always felt like something distant, something for later down the road. But now, watching Jackson study the houses on his screen, his fingers drumming against the counter like he was already picturing it, I started to wonder.

Maybe permanence wasn't as scary as I thought.

"Alright," I said, closing my laptop and turning to him. "Let's look at some houses."

Jackson grinned, pulling up a listing. "This one isn't bad. Three bedrooms, good space, and there's a brewery nearby."

I smirked. "So, we're picking where we live based on alcohol availability?"

He chuckled. "I have my priorities."

Rolling my eyes, I leaned into him, glancing at the listing. The house wasn't massive, but it had charm. It looked like a place where memories could be made, where love could settle into the walls and take root.

"We should schedule a visit," I murmured. "See it in person."

Jackson nodded, his expression serious now. "Yeah. Let's do it."

I felt the certainty settle in my bones. I had never known exactly where I was going, had always worried about making the wrong decisions, but this—this I was sure of.

"You're really sure about this?" I asked quietly, searching his face.

Jackson reached for my hand, threading our fingers together. "I've never been more sure of anything."

I exhaled, nodding. "Then let's do it."

And just like that, the decision was made.

We weren't just moving forward.
We were building something together.

CHAPTER 39

The weekend arrived faster than I expected. The car was packed with snacks, an overnight bag, and a hopeful energy that neither of us acknowledged outright. The drive to the neighboring town was peaceful, the sun warm against the windshield as music played softly in the background. Jackson drummed his fingers on the steering wheel, occasionally glancing at me with a smile that made my heart feel full.

"You nervous?" he asked after a long stretch of silence.

I turned to him, considering the question. "A little. It feels real now."

Jackson nodded. "Yeah. But real doesn't have to be scary."

I reached for his hand, letting our fingers intertwine. "I know."

We arrived at the first home viewing a little early, giving us time to walk around the neighborhood. It was different from the city-quieter, more personal. The kind of place where people nodded in greeting and the air smelled fresher, cleaner.

"It's nice," I admitted as we strolled past a row of coffee shops and boutiques. "Less chaotic than my last apartment before you."

"You mean less chaotic than your apartment with Ceci and three years of noise complaints?" Jackson teased.

I laughed. "Yeah, maybe."

The realty agent met us at the building entrance, giving us a quick rundown before leading us inside. The home was small but open, filled with natural light and the promise of something new. I walked through each room slowly, trying to picture my life here. Our life.

Jackson lingered by the kitchen, opening cabinets like he was already moving in. "You like it?"

I exhaled. "I do. Do you?"

Jackson leaned against the counter, watching me carefully. "If it means waking up next to you every day, yeah."

My chest tightened, and I let myself believe that this wasn't just an idea, wasn't just a daydream. It was happening.

"Let's put in an offer," I said before I could second-guess myself.

Jackson grinned. "Hell yes."

That night, after a celebratory dinner, we checked into a hotel. The room was modest, but I barely noticed because Jackson was there, and that was all I needed.

I lay on the bed, watching him scroll through his phone, still buzzing with excitement. "I can't believe we did that."

Jackson glanced at me. "It was always going to happen. You just needed to catch up."

I smirked. "So you knew all along?"

He rolled onto his side, propping himself up on his elbow. "I knew we were always going to find our way to this. To each other."

I felt something shift inside me, something quiet but unshakable. I reached up, tracing my fingers along his jaw before pulling him down into a slow, deep kiss.

"I love you," I murmured against his lips.

Jackson's fingers trailed through my hair, his voice steady. "I love you more."

I wasn't afraid of what could come next. I was ready for anything, as long as I had Jackson.

We were building something together.

And it felt like home.

Chapter 40

The days following our house offer were filled with a nervous energy that neither Jackson nor I wanted to acknowledge. The wait stretched between us like a thin thread, taut and fragile, ready to snap with either disappointment or relief.

"What if we don't get it?" I mused one afternoon, sitting cross-legged on the couch, my laptop balanced on my thighs.

Jackson, sprawled out beside me, glanced over. "Then we find another place."

I bit my lip, scrolling mindlessly through my emails. "I just... I really want this one."

He reached out, running his hand gently down my arm. "Then it'll happen."

I huffed. "You can't just manifest reality, Jackson."

Jackson smirked. "Sure I can. It's how I got you, isn't it?"

I rolled my eyes but couldn't stop the small smile from creeping onto my lips.

By the end of the week, the call finally came. My heart pounded as I answered, Jackson watching me from across the room, frozen in anticipation.

"Ms. Grace?" the realty agent said. "Congratulations, your offer has been accepted."

For a moment, I could only blink, the words not quite settling in. "Wait- seriously?"

The agent chuckled. "Seriously. When would you like to pick up your keys?"

I turned to Jackson, eyes wide with disbelief. He was already grinning, standing up before I even said a word.

"We got it?" he mouthed.

I nodded rapidly, a giddy laugh bubbling out of me. "We got it!"

Jackson let out a triumphant yell before scooping me up, spinning me in a tight circle. "Told you! Manifestation works, baby!"

I laughed, my arms clinging to him as the realization fully sank in. "We're starting over!"

Jackson set me down gently, his hands cradling my face. "Yeah. We are."

And then he kissed me, deep and lingering, sealing the moment in something more permanent than memory.

Chapter 41

Moving day was chaos. Between the countless boxes, the aching muscles, and Ceci showing up unannounced with champagne and takeout, it was a whirlwind of exhaustion and excitement.

"You guys actually did it," Ceci said, popping the cork on the champagne. "You're real, functioning adults now."

Jackson collapsed onto the floor- our floor, in our house- and let out a groan. "Barely."

I flopped down beside him, stealing the glass Ceci poured. "I don't think my body will ever recover."

Ceci snorted. "You lifted, like, two boxes."

I waved a dismissive hand. "Mental strain is just as exhausting."

Jackson chuckled, glancing around the mess of our new home. "Well, it's done. This is home now."

I glanced around. The house was still a mess- boxes stacked high, furniture yet to be arranged, chaos in every corner. But he was right.

It was home.

Later that night, when the house was quiet and Ceci had gone home, I stood in the middle of our dimly lit living room, taking it all in. Jackson appeared behind me, wrapping his arms around my waist and resting his chin on my shoulder.

"Penny for your thoughts?" he murmured.

I sighed, leaning back into him. "Just... how different everything feels. How different I feel."

Jackson pressed a soft kiss to the side of my neck. "Good different?"

I turned in his arms, looking up at him. "Yeah. The best kind."

He smiled, brushing a strand of hair from my face. "Then here's to everything that comes next."

I met his gaze, feeling a warmth settle deep in my chest. "To everything that comes next."

We weren't just building a life together.

We were already living it.

For once, I wasn't waiting for something to go wrong.

I was ready for everything to go right.

The morning after our first night in the house, I woke up to the sound of Jackson fumbling around in the kitchen. The scent of coffee and something slightly burnt filled the air. I groaned, rolling over and burying my face in the pillow, a slow smile creeping onto my lips.

Jackson appeared in the doorway a moment later, holding two mismatched coffee mugs. "Good morning, homeowner."

I stretched, sitting up as he handed me a mug. "Are we sure this isn't a dream?"

He grinned, sitting on the edge of the bed. "If it is, I'm not waking up."

I took a slow sip, sighing as the warmth spread through me. "So, what's on the agenda today?"

Jackson smirked. "Unpacking? Fixing the leaky faucet? Finding out what that weird smell in the garage is?"

I groaned. "I liked it better when we were just pretending to be homeowners."

Jackson laughed, leaning over to kiss my forehead. "Too late now. We signed the paperwork. This mess is officially ours."

I sighed dramatically but couldn't wipe the grin off my face. This house, this life- it was everything I had never let myself believe I could have.

The next few days were a blur of unpacking, organizing, and realizing just how much work homeownership actually required. Ceci visited with housewarming gifts, including a toolkit she claimed we would "definitely need."

"You two are going to destroy something trying to fix it," she said, handing Jackson the box.

"Zero faith in us," Jackson said, shaking his head. "That hurts, Ceci."

I smirked. "She's not wrong."

Ceci grinned. "Just don't burn the house down, okay?"

One evening, after a long day of setting up the living room, Jackson and I found ourselves sitting on the floor, takeout containers scattered between us.

"It still doesn't feel real," I admitted, glancing around at the half-unpacked boxes and the fresh coat of paint on the walls.

Jackson reached over, taking my hand in his. "It will. Give it time."

I exhaled, squeezing his fingers. "I'm glad it's with you."

Jackson leaned in, pressing a soft kiss to my lips. "Me too."

And as we sat there, in the house we now called home, I realized something: for once in my life, I wasn't looking for an escape.

I was exactly where I was meant to be.

Chapter 42

The following days passed in a blur of half-unpacked boxes, takeout meals, and the endless realization that homeownership came with a never-ending to-do list. Every time we crossed one thing off our list, another issue popped up. The sink dripped, the cabinet doors squeaked, the walls needed another coat of paint.

I stood in the middle of our still-chaotic living room, hands on my hips, surveying the mess. "I thought moving in was the hard part."

Jackson, who was sitting cross-legged on the floor tightening a bolt on one of the dining chairs, let out a short laugh. "Nope. Turns out, now we get to learn how to be plumbers, electricians, and furniture builders all in one."

I smirked, shaking my head. "Great. Because that's totally what I went to college for."

Jackson set his wrench down and stretched, rolling his shoulders back. "We'll figure it out."

I let out a small laugh, wiping dust from my hands. "You say that about everything."

He shot me a lazy grin. "And am I ever wrong?"

I rolled my eyes, but deep down, I knew he had a point. We had figured out so much already- together. That realization warmed me more than I expected.

By the third night, exhaustion had fully set in. The living room was still a mess of unpacked boxes, our dining chairs were half-assembled, and the new coffee table stood at an odd tilt, but none of it mattered. The space wasn't perfect yet, but it was ours.

"I can't believe we own this place," I murmured, running my hand along the bare wall where we had planned to hang artwork but hadn't gotten around to yet.

Jackson walked up behind me, wrapping his arms around my waist and resting his chin on my shoulder. "Feels surreal, huh?"

I nodded. "Yeah. I keep expecting someone to tell us we have to leave. That this isn't really ours."

"It's ours, Jules," he said softly. "No one's taking it away."

I leaned into him, closing my eyes for a moment. The weight of the day pressed into me, but for the first time in a long time, it wasn't the kind of exhaustion that came from running away- it was the kind that came from building something worth staying for.

That night, after another long day of trying to make the house feel like a home, we collapsed onto our mattress. Our bed frame remained in pieces against the bedroom wall, so the mattress lay directly on the floor, surrounded by stacks of books and tangled cords we hadn't yet found places for.

Jackson pulled me into his arms, his breath warm against my temple. "I love you, Jules," he murmured. "Even if you suck at using a drill."

I swatted at his arm playfully but nestled closer. "Love you too. Even if you insist we don't need a professional for literally anything."

Jackson chuckled. "One day, we're gonna laugh about all of this."

I let my eyes drift shut, feeling the steady rise and fall of his chest beneath my cheek. The air smelled faintly of sawdust and the remnants of our takeout dinner, but I didn't care. The chaos, the exhaustion, the little moments of frustration- all of it felt right.

We weren't just building a house. We were building a life.

"We already are," I whispered, a small smile tugging at my lips.

Chapter 43

Days blurred into weeks, and our new house slowly transformed into a home. The walls no longer felt bare, the scent of fresh paint had faded, and our laughter filled the spaces between unpacked boxes. But just as we were settling into our rhythm, reality reminded us that life wasn't always easy.

The storm hit hard that evening, a sudden shift in the air as thunder cracked in the distance. I stood by the window, watching the rain come down in relentless sheets, pounding against the house with an intensity that made me uneasy. The sky flashed white for a brief second before darkness swallowed the neighborhood whole.

"Jackson, the power's out again!" I called from the kitchen, flashlight in hand.

Jackson groaned from the living room, rubbing a hand down his face as he stared at the breaker panel. "Yeah, no kidding. Pretty sure this wiring is older than we are."

I sighed, wrapping my sweater tighter around myself. "How are we supposed to get anything done if we can't even keep the lights on?"

Jackson walked over, pressing a quick kiss to my forehead. "We'll figure it out."

I gave him a pointed look. "You say that about everything."

"And am I ever wrong?" he teased, wiggling his eyebrows.

I smirked despite my frustration, but deep down, I worried. Our house had quirks—more than quirks, really. Faulty wiring, leaky pipes, an ancient water heater, and an ever-growing list of repairs we hadn't budgeted for.

"I don't want to keep patching things up, Jackson. I want this place to be ours, not just some fixer-upper we keep throwing money at."

Jackson sighed, hands on his hips as he looked around. "I know, Jules. We'll get there. One thing at a time."

A loud crack of thunder shook the house, and I flinched. The candlelight flickered, casting long shadows across the walls. The flickering glow made the living room look almost eerie, the walls stretching in unfamiliar ways. I exhaled deeply, watching Jackson's face, his unwavering confidence despite the mess surrounding us.

I wanted to believe him. I really did.

Then, something dripped onto my shoulder.

I frowned and looked up- another drop hit my cheek. A dark stain had spread across the ceiling.

"Jackson..."

He followed my gaze, and his face fell. "You have got to be kidding me."

The ceiling let out a soft creak, and suddenly, water started trickling down the wall, slow at first before forming a steady stream.

"Oh, hell no," Jackson muttered, already moving for a bucket. "If this turns into a flood, we're sleeping in the damn car."

I let out a half-laugh, half-sob. "Home sweet home, right?"

Jackson smirked as he slid a bucket under the leak. "Every homeowner's dream."

And yet, despite the frustration, despite the exhaustion, I felt something else.

This was ours. Our mess. Our storm. And somehow, together, we'd get through it.

Chapter 44

    Juliette was exhausted. Between work, student loans, and the endless stress of homeownership, the weight of it all was settling into my bones. The excitement of moving in had faded into something more complicated, something that made my chest feel heavy at night.

    Meanwhile, Jackson carried it all like it was nothing- like it was just another challenge to tackle, another problem with a solution waiting to be found. But I wasn't so sure.

    I sat curled up on the couch, my laptop balanced on my knees, fingers tapping anxiously against the trackpad as I stared at our bank statements. The glow from the screen was the only source of light in the dimly lit room, casting long shadows against the half-painted walls.

"You're up late," Jackson said, standing in the doorway of our half-finished living room. He ran a towel through his damp hair, fresh from a shower, his shoulders relaxed in a way that made me envy him.

I barely looked up. "Trying to balance the budget."

Jackson frowned, stepping further into the room. "Again? Jules, we'll figure it out."

I let out a sharp laugh, rubbing my temples. "Yeah, because that's worked so well so far."

Jackson hesitated before walking over to sit beside me. The couch groaned under his weight, and for a moment, neither of us spoke.

"What's really going on?" he finally asked, his voice softer now.

I exhaled, staring at the numbers on the screen. "I just... I thought this part would be easier. That once we got here, once we had the house, everything would just fall into place. That it would feel like home right away."

Jackson nodded slowly, his expression unreadable. "Yeah, me too."

The admission caught me off guard. Jackson rarely admitted when things weren't perfect. He was always so sure, so steady. Seeing him admit the struggle somehow made it feel more real- and less like I was failing.

He leaned back, running a hand through his damp hair. "It's overwhelming, I know. The mortgage, the repairs, the bills. But we wanted this, didn't we?"

I chewed on my lip, glancing around the unfinished room, the peeling paint, the faint sound of a dripping faucet in the kitchen. The dream we had once clung to felt farther away than ever, but even in the mess, in the uncertainty, there was something grounding about Jackson's presence.

"Yeah," I said softly. "We did."

Jackson leaned closer, pressing a kiss to my temple. "Then we'll figure it out. Together."

I sighed, closing my laptop and setting it aside. Maybe I didn't have all the answers. Maybe we never would. But if Jackson was still choosing to fight for this, maybe I could too.

I rested my head against his shoulder, letting the weight of the moment settle between us. "I just want it to feel like ours."

Jackson's arm tightened around me. "It already is. We just have to build it one day at a time."

I closed my eyes, exhaling slowly. Maybe I didn't have everything figured out. Maybe the house wasn't quite a home yet. But we were here, together. And maybe, in the end, that was all that mattered.

Chapter 45

  Juliette could feel the stress creeping into every corner of our house, stretching thin between us like an invisible thread ready to snap. The repairs, the bills, the endless to-do lists- it was all starting to add up. And, since moving in, Jackson and I were starting to feel it in each other.

  The next morning, I woke up alone. Jackson had already left for work, leaving a note on the kitchen counter next to a half-drunk cup of coffee.

Running late. Love you. Don't stress too much.

I sighed, rubbing my eyes as I stared at the note. Too late.

By the time Jackson got home that evening, I had already worked myself into frustration. The ceiling leak from the storm had turned into something worse, and I had spent hours researching repair estimates that made my stomach turn. Plus, the lamp kept looking weird to me every time I caught it in the corner of my eye. Almost like it glitched.

Jackson walked in, kicking off his boots by the door. "Hey, babe. What's for dinner?"

I stared at him, incredulous. "Really? That's your first question?"

Jackson blinked, confused. "Uh... yeah?"

I scoffed, tossing a paper onto the table. "The contractor came by today. Wanna guess how much it's going to cost to fix the leak?"

Jackson picked up the paper, his jaw tightening as he skimmed the numbers. "Shit."

"Yeah, shit, Jackson. And that's just the ceiling. We still have to figure out the wiring, the plumbing, and about a dozen other things we don't have the money for."

Jackson ran a hand through his hair, exhaling. "Jules, I know it's a lot, but we'll find a way. We always do."

I let out a humorless laugh. "Right. Because that's worked so well so far."

Jackson frowned. "What's that supposed to mean?"

I threw up my hands. "It means I'm tired, Jackson! Tired of always 'figuring it out.' Tired of always pretending we're fine when we're barely keeping our heads above water."

Jackson was silent for a moment before he spoke, his voice calmer but firm. "We chose this, Jules. We wanted this. It's not supposed to be easy."

I clenched my jaw. "I know that. But wanting something doesn't magically make it work."

Jackson sighed, stepping toward me. "We're not failing, Jules. We're just struggling. There's a difference."

"It doesn't feel like it." My voice was softer now, the exhaustion finally catching up to me.

Jackson reached for my hands, his thumbs brushing over my knuckles. "Then let's take a breath. One thing at a time."

I exhaled, closing my eyes for a moment before nodding. "Okay."

Jackson pulled me into a hug, pressing a kiss on my forehead. "We're gonna be okay." He sealed his promise with a kiss on my lips.

And even though I still wasn't sure, I let myself believe him. Just for tonight.

CHAPTER 46

The tension from that argument didn't disappear overnight. We carried it in quiet ways—in the way I spent extra hours at work, in the way Jackson disappeared into house projects that didn't really need fixing. We weren't fighting, not exactly. But something unspoken sat between us, an invisible weight neither of us acknowledged.

It was in the mornings, when I woke up to find Jackson already gone, leaving behind only half-drunk cups of coffee and notes scribbled on scraps of paper. It was in the way he didn't kiss me as long, in the way I stayed late at work to avoid the inevitable conversations.

One evening, Ceci called, her voice bright despite my exhaustion. "Hey, you alive over there?"

I chuckled, sinking into the couch. "Barely. What's up?"

"Just checking in. You've been MIA."

I hesitated before sighing. "It's just... a lot right now. The house, money, everything."

Ceci was quiet for a moment. "And Jackson?"

I pressed my fingers against my temple. "He's... Jackson. He thinks everything is going to work out if we just keep trying."

Ceci hummed. "And you don't?"

"I don't know," I admitted. "I just feel like we jumped into something we weren't ready for. And now, I don't know if we can keep up."

"But do you still love him?"

My breath hitched. "Of course I do."

"Then talk to him, Jules. Before you start resenting him."

I nodded, even though Ceci couldn't see me. "Yeah. You're right."

After we hung up, I sat in silence for a long time before getting up and searching for Jackson. I found him in the garage, kneeling by his toolbox, pretending to be busy with something that clearly didn't need fixing.

"Hey," I said softly.

Jackson glanced up, his face carefully neutral. "Hey."

I hesitated before stepping closer. "Can we talk?"

He set down his wrench, wiping his hands on his jeans. "Yeah. Let's talk."

I swallowed hard, fiddling with my ring, trying to gather my words. "I know we've been off lately. I don't want to keep pretending everything is fine when it's not."

Jackson leaned against the workbench, crossing his arms. "I don't either. But I don't know what you want me to say, Jules. We're stressed. We're figuring it out. That's just life."

I bit my lip. "I just... I need to know that we're still in this together. That we still want this."

Jackson's face softened. "Of course I want this. I want you. But I don't know how to fix everything overnight."

"I'm not asking you to," I murmured. "I just need to know that when things get hard, you won't shut me out."

Jackson sighed, reaching for my hands. "I won't. I promise."

I exhaled, letting my fingers intertwine with his. "Good. Because I don't want to lose us."

He pulled me into his arms, pressing his forehead to mine. "You won't. We just have to keep choosing each other. Every day."

I let myself believe that maybe, just maybe, we could.

Maybe love wasn't about things being easy. Maybe it was about weathering the storms together, even when the foundation cracked beneath us.

Chapter 47

The conversation in the garage had given us a moment of peace, but it hadn't erased the underlying tension. It lingered, buried beneath reassurances and hopeful words, waiting for the next storm to hit. And it did, in the smallest of ways- little arguments over money, a sigh too heavy, a door shut a little too hard.

I felt it in my bones. The uncertainty. The weight of something unsaid pressing down on us both. I saw it in the way Jackson stayed out later, losing himself in errands that shouldn't have taken hours. In the way he checked his phone more, scrolling mindlessly before setting it down and pretending he hadn't been distracted.

One evening, as we sat at the dinner table- takeout boxes between us, neither making an effort to cook- I finally spoke. "Are you happy?"

Jackson looked up mid-bite, chewing slower than necessary before swallowing. "What?"

I met his gaze, heart pounding. "Are you happy? With this? With us?"

Jackson set his fork down, rubbing a hand over his face. "Jules, what kind of question is that?"

"An honest one."

His sigh was long, measured. "I mean, yeah. I love you. We're just going through a rough patch. That's normal."

"Normal," I echoed, stirring my rice with my chopsticks. "I don't know if it's normal or if we're just pretending it is."

Jackson frowned. "Are you saying you're not happy?"

I hesitated. "I don't know."

The words felt like a betrayal the second they left my mouth, but they were true. I wasn't unhappy, not entirely. But there was an unease in my chest I couldn't shake. Like I was walking on a tightrope, waiting to fall.

Jackson pushed his food aside and leaned forward, resting his elbows on the table. "Okay. Then let's talk about it. What do you need? What's missing?"

I swallowed, trying to piece together an answer. "I don't know if it's about something being missing. I just feel like we're losing something."

Jackson's jaw tightened. "So what, you think we made a mistake? Buying this house? Moving in together?"

"That's not what I'm saying."

"Then what are you saying, Juliette? Because from where I'm sitting, it sounds like you're regretting all of this."

My throat burned. "I'm not regretting us. I just... I don't want us to end up resenting each other because we're trying so hard to make this work that we forget why we wanted it in the first place."

Jackson let out a slow breath, his fingers tapping against the edge of the table. "I don't resent you. And I don't think I ever could."

I looked at him, really looked at him- the man I loved, the man I had chosen. The exhaustion in his eyes mirrored my own. He wasn't the enemy. Neither of us was. But we were tired. And love, as much as I wanted to believe it was enough, didn't magically fix everything.

I reached for his hand. "I don't want to fight you, Jackson. I just want us to be okay."

He squeezed my fingers. "Then let's make sure we are. No more burying things. If something's wrong, we say it. Deal?"

I nodded, a small smile tugging at my lips. "Deal."

The tension didn't vanish. The problems weren't magically solved. But in that moment, there was still love between us.

And maybe, just maybe, that was enough to keep fighting for.

Chapter 48

The next few days were quiet. Not in a comforting way, but in the kind of silence that felt heavy, pressing in on us with every unfinished conversation. Jackson and I went through the motions- waking up, going to work, coming home- but the warmth that used to fill our space had dulled into something muted, something hesitant.

I hated it. I hated how it felt like we were skirting around the inevitable, avoiding the deeper issue neither of us wanted to name. Because naming it would make it real.

One evening, I sat on the back porch, staring out at the overgrown yard, sipping at a glass of wine I didn't really want. The weight of everything felt unbearable, like a storm hovering just beyond the horizon, waiting for the right moment to break.

Jackson finally stepped outside, rubbing the back of his neck as he joined me. He didn't sit right away, just stood there, looking at me like he was trying to read my mind.

"You okay?" he asked.

I huffed out a soft laugh, shaking my head. "That's the second time this week you've asked me that, and I still don't have an answer."

Jackson sighed, dropping into the chair beside me. "I don't know what to say, Jules. I don't know how to make this better."

"Maybe that's the problem," I murmured. "Maybe we keep trying to fix something that isn't broken, just... changing."

Jackson frowned. "I don't want us to change. Not like this."

I took a slow sip of my wine, staring into the deep red liquid as if it held answers. "But we are. Whether we like it or not."

He exhaled sharply, running a hand through his hair. "Then what do we do?"

I turned to him, really looking at him, taking in the exhaustion, the frustration, the love that was still there but felt so much harder to reach. "We stop pretending everything is fine. We stop thinking love is enough to make this easy. Because it's not."

Jackson clenched his jaw. "Are you saying love isn't enough?"

I hesitated. "I'm saying love is work. And I need to know that we're both willing to do that work."

Jackson nodded slowly, considering my words. "I am, Jules. I just... I don't always know how."

I reached for his hand, threading my fingers through his. "Neither do I. But maybe that's okay. Maybe we don't have to know everything right now. We just have to keep trying."

Jackson squeezed my hand. "Then let's try."

For the first time in days, I felt like I could breathe a little easier.

Maybe we weren't falling apart. Maybe we were just learning how to hold on.

Chapter 49

The days moved forward, but the tension lingered like a ghost between us. Some nights, I'd catch Jackson staring at me as if searching for the right words. Other times, he'd brush past me in the kitchen, his touch lingering on my lower back, small gestures that whispered, I'm still here. But we both knew that wasn't enough. Not yet.

One evening, I came home late from work, exhausted. The weight of the day clung to my shoulders, pressing down as I stepped inside. The smell of something warm and familiar filled the house- garlic, herbs, something simmering on the stove. I followed it to the kitchen, where

Jackson stood, stirring a pot of pasta sauce, his brow furrowed in focus.

"You cooked?" I asked, surprised.

Jackson glanced over his shoulder, a small, almost shy smile pulling at his lips. "Figured we could use a real meal for once."

I hesitated before stepping forward, placing my bag on the counter. "It smells amazing."

"Tastes better," he said, grabbing a spoon and offering me a taste.

I leaned in, letting the rich flavor settle on my tongue. "Damn. When did you learn to cook like this?"

Jackson smirked. "YouTube."

I laughed, shaking my head. "I love that."

His expression softened. "I love you."

The words hung between us, heavier than usual, weighted with all the unspoken fears and the stubborn hope we hadn't quite let go of.

I exhaled. "I love you, too."

We ate together, sitting at the dining table instead of the couch, the way we used to before everything got hard. The conversation was light, easy- memories of when we first started dating, stories of dumb mistakes we'd made in the house already. It felt... good. Not perfect, but something close.

Later, as we curled into bed, Jackson wrapped his arms around me from behind, his breath warm against my neck. "We're going to be okay, Jules."

I didn't respond right away, letting the words settle in my chest, grounding me.

"I know," I whispered finally, turning in his arms to press a kiss against his lips. "As long as we keep trying."

And in that moment, I believed it. Maybe love wasn't about being perfect together- maybe it was about choosing each other, even when everything felt messy. Maybe the cracks didn't mean we were breaking.

Maybe we were just letting the light in.

Chapter 50

The decision to take a trip had been impulsive. After weeks of tension, late-night conversations, and half-hearted reassurances, Jackson suggested we get away- just the two of us, no work, no bills, no house projects looming over us. I had hesitated at first, but the thought of escaping, even for a few days, was too tempting to resist.

"A road trip?" I asked, arching a brow. "Where to?"

Jackson had simply shrugged. "Anywhere but here."

So we packed our bags, threw them into the trunk of Jackson's old car, and hit the road before dawn. The highway stretched endlessly before us, a ribbon of asphalt leading to nowhere in particular. We didn't have a plan- just a full tank of gas and the unspoken hope that this trip would somehow fix the cracks neither of us fully knew how to repair.

At first, things felt lighter. I watched as Jackson drummed his fingers on the steering wheel, humming along to the music playing through the crackling speakers. The tension that had coiled in my chest for weeks finally began to loosen.

"This reminds me of that trip we took a few months ago," I mused, my fingers idly tracing the curve of my knee.

Jackson smirked. "The one where we got lost for three hours because you swore you didn't need the GPS?"

I gasped in mock offense. "I was navigating from my gut, okay?"

"Your gut was wrong."

"My gut was adventurous," I corrected. "There's a difference."

Jackson chuckled, shaking his head. "If you say so."

For a while, it felt good. Easy. Like we had stepped back into a version of ourselves that existed before the house, before the stress, before the weight of adulthood had settled on our shoulders. We stopped at small roadside diners, laughed at stupid billboards, and talked about anything but our problems.

Then the rain started.

It was light at first- just a mist, barely enough to flick on the wipers. But within an hour, it had transformed into a downpour, sheets of water blurring the windshield, the wipers struggling to keep up. The road stretched dark and slick beneath us, the sky a swirling mass of gray.

"We should pull over," I suggested, gripping the armrest as a truck sped past us, spraying a wave of water onto the windshield.

Jackson shook his head, eyes locked on the road. "There's nowhere to stop. We're in the middle of nowhere."

A pit formed in my stomach. The road was barely visible now, the headlights reflecting off the glistening pavement. I stole a glance at Jackson- his jaw was tight, his knuckles white against the steering wheel.

"Maybe we should turn around? Find a motel and wait it out?" I tried again.

Jackson sighed. "We'll be fine. Just a little rain."

But it wasn't just a little rain. It was a storm, the kind that swallowed the sky and made everything feel smaller, more fragile. The car's tires skidded slightly as Jackson rounded a curve, and my breath caught in my throat.

"Jackson- "

The moment stretched, elongated by the sharp screech of tires losing grip, the blinding flash of headlights from the opposite lane, the sickening feeling of weightlessness as the car hydroplaned.

Then- impact.

A violent jolt. Metal crumpling. The world spinning in chaotic disarray.

My scream was swallowed by the deafening crash, the sound of glass shattering, the world tilting sideways. And then-

Darkness.

Silence.

Nothing.

Chapter 51

A beeping noise. Faint, rhythmic, persistent.

My eyelids felt impossibly heavy, my body weighed down as though I were sinking into something thick and suffocating. The air around me smelled sterile- antiseptic, faint traces of something metallic. A low hum of voices swirled at the edge of my consciousness, muffled and distant.

Then, a voice cut through. "Juliette? Jules? Oh my God- can you hear me?"

Ceci.

My fingers twitched. Then my breath stuttered, my body reacting before my mind fully caught up. A sharp inhale burned my lungs, my throat raw and dry, as if I hadn't used it in months. Slowly, painfully, I pried my eyes open.

Blinding light. White walls. Machines surrounding me, tubes running from my arms.

Hospital.

A strangled noise caught in my throat as I tried to sit up, but my limbs refused to cooperate. Panic clawed its way through my chest.

"Hey, hey, easy- " Ceci was beside me in an instant, hands gripping mine. "It's okay, Jules. Just breathe. You're safe."

I swallowed hard, my gaze darting around the room. "Where's Jackson?"

Ceci's expression faltered, her brows knitting together. "Who?"

My chest tightened. "Jackson," I repeated, trying to push through the thick fog in my brain. "Where is he? He- he was with me. We were on a trip. We- we bought a house."

Ceci's fingers squeezed mine, grounding me. "Jules... I don't know who you're talking about."

My breath hitched. "What do you mean? He's- he's my fiancé. He was with me when- "

The moment stretched too long, Ceci's silence pressing in on me like a vise. There was something unreadable in her eyes, something hesitant, like she was treading carefully over broken glass.

"Jules..." Ceci's voice was soft, deliberate. "You've been in a coma for six months. You were in a car accident."

I blinked, the words colliding in my brain, unable to take shape. "No," I whispered. "No, that's not right."

Ceci's eyes filled with something that looked like heartbreak. "It is. You and Cory were in an accident. He... he didn't make it."

My stomach lurched, nausea rising so fast I thought I might choke on it. "I know that. I know Cory died- I was at his funeral."

Ceci hesitated, looking at me carefully. "Jules... you weren't there. You've been here the whole time."

I shook my head, my pulse hammering in my ears. "No. No, I woke up. I grieved. I moved on. Jackson- " My voice broke, the weight of my own certainty crumbling beneath me. "Jackson was real."

Ceci swallowed hard, her expression stricken. "Jules... there is no Jackson. I never heard you talk about him before."

The words barely registered at first. They didn't make sense. They didn't fit into the life I remembered- the life I lived. The late-night talks, the fights, the whispered promises. The future we planned together.

Real. It had been real.

Hadn't it?

My breath came in sharp gasps, panic blooming as I clawed through the memories, trying to find something solid, something undeniable. But the more I searched, the more it all fell apart. The edges blurred, the details twisted, reshaping themselves into something that no longer made sense.

Jackson had never existed.

My mind reeled, desperate to understand, desperate to latch onto something real. "No. No, I loved him. I knew him. He was real. He- "

My voice cracked, my body trembling as the truth crashed over me like a tidal wave, pulling me under. I had created him. A mind desperate for something to hold onto, something to keep me alive while my body remained trapped in the darkness. A figment. A lifeline. Nothing more.

My entire love story had been a dream.

Ceci's arms wrapped around me as I broke, my sobs wracking through my frail body. "I'm so sorry, Jules," she murmured, her own voice shaking. "I don't know why your mind did this. I don't know why it gave you him. But I'm here. I'm real. And I'm not going anywhere."

I clung to her, gasping for air, for understanding, for anything that could make this hurt less.

But nothing could soften the devastation of waking up and realizing the only thing keeping me alive... was never real at all.

Chapter 52

The hospital room was quiet except for the steady beeping of the monitors and the occasional rustling of Ceci shifting in the chair beside my bed. The weight of the truth pressed down on my chest, heavier than the blankets draped over my fragile frame. I felt hollow, like a ghost of myself lingering in a world that no longer made sense.

Jackson had never existed.

My fingers traced the crease of my hospital gown absentmindedly, my mind still fighting against the reality of it all. The memories of him felt so real- his laugh, the way his arms felt around me, the warmth of his hand in mine. And yet, they were nothing. A trick my subconscious had played to keep me tethered to life while my body lay motionless for months.

I swallowed hard, blinking up at the sterile ceiling. "I don't know how to exist without him."

Ceci exhaled slowly, reaching for my hand. "You do exist, Jules. You always did. He was never real, but you are. You survived."

I let out a dry, humorless laugh. "Survived what? A dream? Because right now, it feels like I lost everything."

Ceci's expression softened, but she didn't argue. Instead, she squeezed my fingers gently. "I won't pretend to know what you're feeling. But I do know that you're still here. And that has to mean something."

I wanted to believe that. I wanted to believe that I wasn't just a shell of the girl who had fallen in love with someone who never existed. But if Jackson was a fabrication of my mind, what did that say about me? About the life I thought I had built? Had I been so desperate for love, for stability, that I had created it out of nothing?

"What was real?" I whispered. "What part of me wasn't a lie?"

Ceci shook her head. "Everything else. You were real. The things you felt? They were real. Even if Jackson wasn't."

I squeezed my eyes shut, fresh tears slipping free. "It hurts."

Ceci pulled me into a hug, careful not to disturb the IV in my arm. "I know. And it will for a while. But you're going to be okay."

I wasn't sure I believed that, but I nodded anyway. Because I had to start somewhere.

The first time I stood on my own, my legs threatened to buckle beneath me. The world spun, my body still adjusting to movement after months of stillness. Ceci was at my side in an instant, steadying me.

"I've got you," she murmured.

I exhaled shakily, gripping her arm. "I feel like I'm learning how to live again."

Ceci smiled, though her eyes were filled with something deeper- understanding. "Maybe you are. But that's okay. One step at a time."

So I took one. Then another. And though the weight of loss still sat heavy in my chest, I kept moving.

Because for once in my life, I was learning how to exist for myself.

Weeks passed in a haze of physical therapy and restless nights haunted by dreams of a man who never was. My muscles screamed in protest every time I tried to walk across the sterile hospital floors, but I pushed through. I needed to feel something other than the ache of absence.

"You're getting stronger," the physical therapist said one afternoon as I limped along the parallel bars. "Give it time."

Time. The concept felt foreign. I had lived an entire life inside my mind in what should have been empty, uncounted hours. Time had lost its meaning the moment my car hydroplaned off that rain-slicked road.

That night, I sat by the window, watching the rain trickle down the glass. The night sky mirrored the confusion inside me- dark, vast, and unknowable. Ceci sat in the chair beside me, scrolling through her phone.

"Do you remember when we used to sit on the apartment balcony and talk about everything and nothing?" I asked softly.

Ceci looked up and smiled faintly. "Of course. We had big plans. Thought we'd conquer the world."

"Yeah," I said, my voice hollow. "And look at me now. I'm barely holding myself together."

Ceci set down her phone and leaned forward. "Jules, you went through something unimaginable. Your mind tried to protect you. That doesn't make you weak. It makes you a survivor."

I shook my head, my eyes burning. "I built an entire relationship in my head. I fell in love with someone who wasn't real. I planned a future that never existed. How do I move on from that? How do I trust what's real now?"

Ceci took my hand, her grip firm. "One day at a time. One truth at a time. I'm real. This moment is real. Start with that."

I looked at her, searching for the certainty she seemed so sure of. The warmth of her hand in mine was solid, undeniable. Real.

"Okay," I whispered. "One day at a time."

The day I was discharged, the air outside felt too sharp, too loud, after months of hospital quiet. The world hadn't stopped while I was gone; it had simply moved on without me.

Ceci helped me into the passenger seat of her car, adjusting the seatbelt across my chest. "Ready?"

"Not really," I admitted.

She gave me a reassuring smile. "That's okay. We'll figure it out."

The car ride home was a blur of unfamiliar familiarity. The streets I once knew by heart now seemed foreign. When we pulled into the parking lot of my apartment building, I hesitated before opening the door.

"What if it still feels like I'm dreaming?" I asked.

Ceci squeezed my hand. "Then we'll remind you what's real."

Stepping inside, the smell of stale air and unopened mail greeted me. Everything was exactly as I'd left it, yet it all felt wrong. My gaze landed on the couch where I remembered watching movies with Jackson. I flinched.

"I don't know if I can do this."

Ceci came to stand beside me. "You don't have to do it alone."

I nodded, tears blurring my vision. I had lost Jackson, but I still had Ceci. I still had myself.

And somehow, that would have to be enough.

Epilogue

Weeks passed. Seasons shifted. The ache of loss dulled but never fully disappeared. I had spent so long living in a world that didn't exist, and now, each day felt like a fragile attempt at rebuilding something I wasn't sure how to name.

I worked. I went home with Ceci. I tried to sleep without dreaming of a face that had never been real.

One night, after a long shift at the bar, I was wiping down the counter, lost in thought, when the bell above the door chimed. I didn't look up at first—just another late-night customer stopping in before closing.

"Hey, sorry," a deep voice said. "Didn't realize you were about to lock up. Just needed a drink after work."

Something in the air changed. I froze, fingers tightening around the cloth in my hand.

That voice. The rhythm of it. The familiarity that made my stomach twist in ways I couldn't explain.

Slowly, I lifted my gaze—and felt the breath leave my body.

He looked exactly like Jackson.

Tall, dark-haired, those same deep brown eyes framed by thick lashes. My mind screamed that it wasn't possible, that this was just another trick, another cruel manifestation of the past.

The man gave me a small, tired smile and slid onto a stool. "Long day?"

I swallowed hard, forcing myself to breathe. "You could say that."

I studied him carefully. He had the same quiet confidence, the same easy presence. But there was something else—something different in the way he carried himself.

"Whiskey neat?" I asked, falling into routine to steady myself.

He chuckled. "How'd you know?"

I managed a small smile. "Lucky guess."

As I poured the drink, he held out his hand. "I'm Adrian, by the way."

My fingers hesitated for only a second before I took it. His grip was warm, steady, real.

"Juliette."

Author's Note

Writing this book has been an emotional journey- one of healing, growth, and endless late nights fueled by caffeine and creativity. I could not have completed it without the unwavering support of the people in my life.

To Dylan- my partner, my true love, and my greatest supporter. Thank you for always believing in me, grounding me when I lose myself in the whirlwind of my imagination, and reminding me that reality holds its own kind of magic. Your faith in me means more than words can say.

To my family and friends- thank you for being my foundation. Your encouragement lifted me during moments of doubt, and your belief in me kept me pushing forward, even when the path seemed impossible.

To my friends- who patiently endured countless conversations about plot twists, character arcs, and the endless "what if" scenarios- thank you for your excitement, your insights, and for never telling me to shut up (even though you probably should have).

To Jacob- you left a mark on my heart that will never fade. Your friendship, your laughter, and your spirit live on in these pages and in me. Thank you for being part of my story, even when you could no longer be here to read it. This book carries pieces of you with every word.

And to my readers- thank you for stepping into these worlds with me, for embracing every twist and turn, and for letting these characters find a home in your hearts. Your support is the greatest gift I could ask for.

With love (and an infinite supply of coffee!),

Allasandra Buckner

Made in the USA
Coppell, TX
06 April 2025

47977592R00144